EP DZ

W9-AWK-092

"Can you handle her?"

"Got her," Barrett said as his large hand weaved beneath the baby, cradled her head and lifted her up. Then, almost immediately, he placed her on the bed.

To his credit, the man was totally attentive to the child. Zoey stood there a few seconds just watching the way he seemed to be studying every inch of his infant daughter. He appeared curious, as if she was some alien creature. He traced the tiny outline of her mouth with his fingers.

"Oh, Miss Kincade," Barrett called out as Zoey turned to leave the room. "We have a slight problem here."

"We do?"

"Actually," he sighed irritably, "*you* have a problem."

"I do?"

"Most definitely. You see, my dear, this isn't my child."

Dear Reader,

Imagine waking up from a six-month-long coma and finding out you've become a father...*and* that the baby put in your arms is not the right one!

So begins *The Baby Exchange* by bestselling Intrigue author Kelsey Roberts. It's the second book of the LOST & FOUND trilogy, started last month by Dani Sinclair. In each book, you'll follow the footsteps of one mystery baby or another's tiny footsteps through a maze of intrigue.

Don't miss the continuing story, *A Baby to Love* by Susan Kearney, next month.

Regards,

Debra Matteucci
Senior Editor and Editorial Coordinator
Harlequin Books
300 East 42nd Street
New York, New York 10017

The Baby Exchange
Kelsey Roberts

Harlequin Books

**TORONTO • NEW YORK • LONDON
AMSTERDAM • PARIS • SYDNEY • HAMBURG
STOCKHOLM • ATHENS • TOKYO • MILAN
MADRID • WARSAW • BUDAPEST • AUCKLAND**

With great thanks to Dani Sinclair for letting me play with her baby.

ISBN 0-373-22374-9

THE BABY EXCHANGE

Copyright © 1996 by Rhonda Harding-Pollero

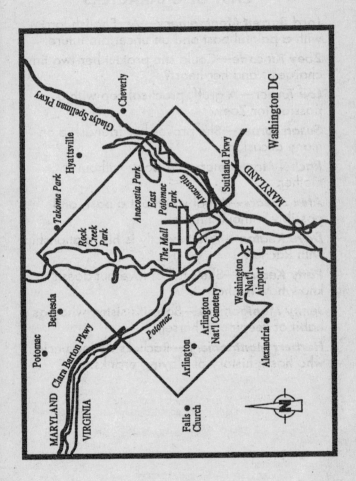

CAST OF CHARACTERS

Lord Barrett Montgomery—An English lord with a painful past and an uncertain future.

Zoey Kincade—Could she protect her two tiny charges...and her heart?

Lou Turner—A gruff, practical cop with a passion for Zoey.

Susan Turner—She proves her friendship on many occasions.

Rachel Montgomery—A baby without a mother.

Alex Spears—A baby without a past, and possibly without a future.

Dave Keaton—What exactly is his relationship with Rachel?

Patty Keaton—She's full of love but doesn't know how to show it.

Jenny Montgomery—Barrett's sister, who has a habit of keeping to herself.

Herbert Montgomery—Rachel's doting uncle, who has a history of playing pranks.

Chapter One

"Please don't cry," Zoey Kincade pleaded as she wrestled a very wiggly Alex into his car seat.

The perspiration on her brow wasn't a result of the sultry summer day or the famous District of Columbia humidity. Nope, her current state of physical exhaustion and distress was directly attributable to the wailing two-month-old she was attempting to settle. Alex had been up half the night, rubbing his nose with his fists. She'd checked his temperature, his diaper, his crib, all in vain. It was just one of those nights. Of course, with two babies under one roof, many of her nights were disasters.

"Hold still," she pleaded until she was able to insert the shiny metal lock of the car seat into place. "One down," she said on a sigh, then dashed into her apartment, grabbed Rachel and raced back to the car.

Little Rachel was nothing like her male counterpart. She was the ideal baby, even-tempered and very adaptable. "Today is your special day," she told the tiny girl. "That's why I dressed you in all this itchy lace," she explained as she tried to fold the stiff collar away from the baby's round face. "As soon as you finish visiting with your daddy, I promise I'll take these absurd clothes off you." The baby's dark blue eyes followed Zoey's movements. "You may as well learn early on that girl clothes can be uncomfortable."

With Rachel and Alex strapped in the back seat, Zoey slipped behind the wheel and tilted down the mirror so she could see herself. "Why didn't one of you tell me that I'd put mascara on only one eye?" she groaned.

Alex's response was predictable. He let out a scream that almost immediately evolved into an angry, body-wrenching series of sobs.

"Calm down, honey. We're not going to be in the nasty car for very long."

Apparently, Alex didn't care for her assurances. He continued to cry, and it wasn't long before Rachel joined in. Zoey tried talking to them, she tried the radio, she tried singing, she even tried to drive and reach behind her to jiggle a car seat at the same time.

The dynamic duo was unrelenting. The seven-mile trip to the hospital quickly deteriorated into a screaming marathon. Her only salvation was that they were too small to really generate much volume. Rachel was almost a month older than Alex but she was small, which made the two look almost like twins. In fact, in the three weeks Zoey had had both babies, she'd found that most people mistook them for twins whenever she ventured out of the house. However, with two infants in tow, she didn't venture out often. Since becoming a foster parent, she hadn't been much of anywhere. This morning's disaster was the reason why.

Zoey had always prided herself on looking professional. Ever since the babies had come into her life, though, she was lucky to get both her legs shaved on the same day. Her once-orderly life was now in total chaos. And she was loving every minute of it. Unlike her previous position, she now felt as if she was actually going to make a difference.

"Okay," she said as she pulled into the parking lot across from Shady Grove Adventist Hospital and flipped the button to open her trunk. An unpleasant, all-too-familiar stench reached her nose. "No, Alex. Please tell me you didn't."

Zoey jumped out and yanked open the back passenger's door. "You did," she groaned, looking at the mess. She reached into the diaper bag and pulled out a box of wipes. "Poor thing...I'm starting to think you have an eating disorder." She began cleaning where he had spit up. Alex's tiny blue eyes remained fixed on her, his expression tugging at her heart. She stopped her chore long enough to caress the soft fuzz on the top of his head. "You can't help it," she said softly. "The doctor says you'll outgrow this vomiting thing when you're bigger. Soon, you'll be like—"

She halted in midsentence when she looked at Rachel. Unfortunately, the poor child had been right in the path of Alex's latest bout of projectile vomiting. The pink dress with the frilly collar and the matching lace headband were a total loss. Sighing, she acknowledged it was going to be a very long morning.

Zoey loaded the babies into the double stroller and took them into the hospital. The staff was kind enough to help her clean up the children before she took them upstairs so Rachel could enjoy the long-awaited reunion with her father. The man had finally awakened from his coma.

Alex's mother was also at Shady Grove, but she wasn't as lucky. As a result of a mugging, she was lingering between life and death, completely dependent upon machines and medicines to keep her alive.

Zoey left the rest room with her two charges, both of whom had been stripped down to their diapers. So much for getting them all spruced up, she thought as she maneuvered her way into the elevator. Alex was happy, finally. He lay there staring up at the overhead lights, his eyes wide, his expression serene. Rachel was her usual calm self, sleeping soundly. Zoey wondered how the baby could be so laid-back given the incredible turmoil she'd endured in her short lifetime.

"How darling," the duty nurse gushed as Zoey wheeled the stroller onto the floor.

She introduced herself and leaned against the counter while a small group of hospital employees took turns holding the babies. She allowed them to be passed from person to person, taking full advantage of the helping hands.

"You don't look anything like your daddy," one of the nurses was saying. "Maybe a little bit, as far as the coloring."

"Right, Debbie. You were paying attention to his coloring."

The two women exchanged conspiratorial looks, then proceeded to fan themselves. "When it comes to that man, I pay attention to *every* detail."

"He's attractive?" Zoey asked. She wasn't all that curious, she was just a little desperate for some adult conversation.

"No. He's gorgeous. He's divine. He's—"

"Enough," the second nurse cut in. "He's a patient. We shouldn't be talking about him like this."

"Okay," the first nurse said as she handed the baby to Zoey. "He's in 712. Lord Barrett Montgomery is something to be viewed, savored and appreciated. But go judge for yourself."

"What should I do with Alex while I'm in his room?"

"We'll keep an eye on this one," the nurse offered, cuddling the little boy against her body.

Zoey was still smiling at the nurses' chatter as she made her way down the brightly lit hallway. The muffled sounds of conversation filtered out from behind partially closed doors. Shifting the sleeping baby up onto her shoulder, she felt herself relax a little. The past month had taken its toll. There was the new career, the cramped new apartment *and* the babies. She tried to remember the last time she'd gotten a full night's sleep.

The door to Lord Montgomery's room was closed. She frowned, wondering why the man wasn't hovering in the doorway waiting anxiously to be with his baby. He hadn't seen his daughter since the first foster family had brought her by, and Zoey had gone to great lengths to arrange this visit. Her disapproval of Lord Montgomery strengthened.

Lifting her hand, she was about to knock just as the door swung wide. Startled, she stepped to the side as a tall, willowy woman clad in a standard-issue white uniform came barreling out.

"Excuse me," the nurse mumbled, reaching out a hand to steady Zoey.

"No harm done," she told the nurse. Zoey patted the still-sleeping baby and smiled at the woman.

Her smile froze on her face when she looked into the room. He was standing in profile by the window, apparently studying something below. A dark, plush robe hung from massive shoulders. The belt rode his hips, outlining his taut stomach and trim waist. He was tall, really tall, even taller than the IV pole guarding him. She stood motionless, watching the small muscles at the side of his mouth twitch nervously. She decided his coloring was pretty good for a man who had endured a terrible accident, a stabbing, a coma and subsequent surgery. His skin still held a faint bronzing from the sun. Her gaze was drawn to the bandage taped neatly near his temple. Above the bandage, his brown hair was mussed, as if he'd been running his hands through the thick mass. Sunlight filtering in from the window revealed reddish highlights, which made Zoey wonder if Rachel would be lucky enough to inherit that beautiful amber shade.

The thought went out of her head the instant he turned and fixed his eyes on her. She could only liken that experience to that time in the fifth grade, when one of the boys had accidentally hit her in the stomach. Her breath seemed to be trapped inside her body.

His eyes were almost as dark as his hair and they were rimmed by long, inky lashes. But it wasn't the size, color or intensity of his eyes that got to her, it was the pain she saw in their chocolaty depths.

"Hi," she said after the brief, awkward pause. Then, moving into the room, she carefully lifted the baby off her shoulder.

The man's expression hardened as he used his thumb to stroke the sleeping child's cheek. It was a tentative, almost fearful touch. It was as if he didn't have the first clue when it came to babies.

"She looks so different," he said in a voice that caught her totally off guard. His proper British accent was delivered in a deep, velvety tone.

"She looked a lot better before Alex barfed all over her," Zoey admitted sheepishly.

"Alex?"

Swallowing the effect his richly accented speech had on her, she offered a small, embarrassed grin. "He's my other baby."

He lifted his eyes to hers and asked, "Yours?"

Zoey felt her cheeks grow warm and she was suddenly aware that mere inches separated her from this man. She was close enough for the clean scent of his shampoo to reach her. Close enough to hear the soft rustling of his hospital gown beneath the expertly monogrammed robe. She was also aware of the fact that he seemed more interested in checking her out than in seeing his baby for the first time in weeks.

"No," she finally answered, her blush deepening. "He's only with me until his mother recovers."

His reaction to her explanation was immediate and telling. Watching his change of expression was like watching a steel door close and lock. He seemed uncomfortable, distant and rigid.

"What happened to her?" he asked, though she didn't get any sense that he was truly interested.

"Alex has a habit of throwing up after he eats. Rachel was just unfortunate enough to—"

"Not Rachel," he interrupted. "The other baby's mother."

"Oh," Zoey answered. She wanted to tell him that his concern should be with his daughter. Why wasn't he asking about Rachel? Her opinion of this man was slipping with each passing second. "She was mugged. The prognosis isn't very good."

"That's unfortunate." He paused then met her eyes and said, "So today is visiting day?"

The teasing light in his eyes caused her heart to flutter ever so slightly. His reaction seemed so inappropriate, and she stumbled through her response. "Something like that. Alex's mom is still unconscious, so he's pretty much just along for the ride."

Barrett kept focusing on her and not his daughter, as if he was comfortable with Zoey but not with his own child. What a cruddy father, she thought. Feeling clumsy standing there holding his baby, she thrust the sleeping infant forward, her knuckles brushing the hardness of his chest. The contact was slight, but it was enough to cause a definite tingle the full length of her arm. "Here, Mr. Montgomery...I mean, sire...or is it—"

"Barrett."

Zoey felt like a total idiot. She had known that Rachel's father was some variety of British royalty, but she hadn't expected this young, handsome, obscenely attractive man. Weren't all the royals stiff, stodgy men that walked with their hands clasped behind their backs? "Okay...Barrett," she finally replied. "You visit with Rachel for a while and I'll just hang out near the nurses' station with Alex."

He seemed apprehensive before he managed his rather snooty response. "As you wish."

"Can you handle her?" Zoey asked, her eyes fixed on the chipped tile floor. For some reason, she felt safer when she wasn't on the receiving end of his piercing gaze.

"Got her," Barrett said as his large hand weaved beneath the baby, cradled her head and lifted her. Then, almost immediately, he placed her on the bed.

Zoey wanted to tell him that babies, particularly his baby, preferred to be held and cuddled. But something told her that this man wouldn't have the faintest notion how to cuddle anything. There was something so reserved, so standoffish about him. He definitely wouldn't be anyone's idea of father of the year.

The baby stirred, her small arms and legs flailing against the air. To his small credit, the man was suddenly totally attentive to the child. She stood there for a few seconds watching the way he seemed to be studying every inch of his infant daughter. He appeared curious, as if Rachel were some creature completely unknown to mankind. He traced the tiny outline of her mouth with his fingers while he gently ran his palm across the curve of her tiny head.

"Then I'll be down the hall," she said, beginning to leave. "Or roaming the halls if Alex gets antsy," she called out as she turned for the door.

"Fine," Barrett answered. "There's only one problem."

"Would you rather I stayed here?" she asked, facing him.

"No," he answered, one dark eyebrow arching up toward the square white bandage.

"Do you need a nurse? Are you feeling okay?"

"I'm fine," he said calmly.

"Then what?"

"We have a slight problem," he said as he stiffened his spine.

"We do?"

"Actually—" he sighed irritably "—*you* have a problem, Miss Kincade."

"I do?"

"Most definitely. You see, my dear, this isn't my baby."

Chapter Two

"The wrong baby?" Zoey gasped.

He moved his head guardedly in deference to his injuries. "It would appear so," he answered. "Do come and look."

As part of his inspection of the baby, Barrett had peeled back the tapes on her diaper. The two-month-old nestled in the folds of the stark white bedding was definitely not Rachel.

"Can you explain this?" he asked, clearly annoyed.

Zoey nodded. "I'm really sorry," she said on a rush of breath. "I guess I got the two of them mixed up when the nurses were passing them back and forth. This is Alex. Rachel is down at the nurses' station."

As she moved to gather up the baby, she was keenly aware of the man standing at her side. She seemed unable to banish the thought that his solid thigh was mere inches from her own. Without even turning her head, she knew he was watching her every move. She could feel it. That knowledge made her nervous and that nervousness must have conveyed itself to her charge. Alex grunted twice, then began to cry in earnest.

She expected the man to hit the roof. Had their positions been reversed, she'd be frantic to see her child. Barrett's demeanor communicated nothing more than mild irritation. As though she'd typed a memo incorrectly instead of bringing him someone else's baby.

"Shush," she said as she picked up Alex. She rocked and swayed in an attempt to soothe the crying baby. As usual, Alex wasn't having any of it.

"Is he always this unhappy?" Barrett asked, his irritation growing.

"Only when I'm around," she admitted as she continued her futile efforts. "I'm learning that this baby isn't very fond of me."

"That must be difficult, given your profession."

Tilting her head, Zoey glanced up at him through the veil of her lashes. So long as he wasn't looking at the baby, his smile was warm, compassionate and fully capable of taking the starch out of her legs.

Alex's wails were abating and his tiny body no longer felt stiff and agitated. "This isn't really my profession."

His dark eyebrows drew together. "Since you've managed to misplace my daughter, informing me that you are not a child-care professional is not exactly of comfort."

Zoey was so taken by his proper, accented speech that she dispensed with the idea of telling him exactly what she thought of him. Lifting Alex so that he was in his favorite position, his head above her shoulder, Zoey met Barrett's warm brown eyes. Rachel's newborn blue eyes had been getting darker almost daily, and now she knew why. The little girl was going to be blessed, in all likelihood, with eyes the color of expensive gourmet coffee.

"I am an elementary-school teacher, Lord Montgomery."

"That's heartening," he responded dryly. "Though I don't believe my daughter is quite ready for formal education."

She watched as he raked square-tipped fingers through the unruly mass of hair. His large hands were contrasted by neatly trimmed and buffed nails. The nails definitely went with the robe. On closer inspection, she guessed the robe cost roughly the equivalent of her monthly budget.

"I've just recently become a part of the foster-care system," she continued. "In addition to my bachelor's degree, I've done some work toward a master's degree in early childhood."

For some reason, she felt it was important to convey to this man that she was a competent, intelligent woman. This man who exuded confidence and success. It was in his body language, in the measure of arrogance with which he held his angled chin. He was the kind of person who could alternately make you feel like the most important human being on the face of the earth, or make you feel as insignificant as a slug. Given that only one of her legs was shaved, Zoey felt a kinship to the lowly slug.

"So what have you done with my daughter?"

"Confused her with Alex," Zoey answered honestly, struggling to keep her shoulders straight and confident. "They look so much alike that it's easy to get them mixed up."

"Then you're obviously not very proficient at your job, Miss Kincade."

"Actually, I am," she told him, imitating the propriety of his tone. "And you can call me Zoey," she added. She didn't necessarily want to be on a first-name basis with a man she didn't hold in high esteem, but she wasn't terribly fond of the way he said her name. It sounded almost like a curse when it fell from his lips.

He frowned. "That's a rather unusual name."

She thought about saying something like "And I'm an unusual woman," but she knew that would sound far too flirtatious. Flirting wasn't professional, and something told her flirting with a man like Barrett Montgomery could be downright dangerous.

"Well?"

"I have never misplaced her before, if that's any consolation. You have to understand how difficult it is to manage two babies at one time." Zoey gently patted Alex's back. "I'm an emergency care-giver. Mostly short-term stuff."

"My daughter is considered an emergency case?"

Zoey nodded. "You were the one who demanded Rachel be removed from the Keatons' care immediately." She averted her eyes, knowing full well that her personal feelings about Rachel's welfare were threatening to enter into the conversation. She knew from the records that Barrett Montgomery was worth a fortune. She had always wondered why a man with unlimited financial resources would allow his daughter to be placed in the foster-care system.

"And Alex?"

"Alex has a problem with projectile vomiting. He's been in three different homes and—"

"No one wanted him?"

Just as you apparently didn't want your own daughter, she remarked silently. Her uncharitable thoughts kept her from answering the question directly. "It is very difficult to find appropriate homes for many of the children. This program was designed to see that none of these kids slipped through the cracks." It wasn't designed as a baby-sitting service for lousy fathers, she fumed quietly.

"Is there a problem?" he asked.

"No, no problem," she lied.

"You appear hostile."

Lifting her chin, she looked directly into his eyes. "I guess I'm just tired, Lord Montgomery. Caring for two infants is very difficult at times. Rewarding," she emphasized, "but difficult."

After several long seconds of tense silence, Zoey said, "I'll run down and get Rachel. I'm sorry for any inconvenience."

Zoey had reached the door, when he called out her name. She stopped but didn't turn around.

"I'm very appreciative of your efforts regarding my daughter's care. I apologize if I sounded judgmental."

"Don't give it a thought," she said quickly. The unexpected praise chased her from the room. Especially when she again felt tempted to tell him what she thought of him. Zoey had come to the hospital with a very low opinion of Lord Montgomery. His behavior hadn't done much to improve that opinion.

HE WATCHED her hasty retreat while taking in deep breaths filled with the lilac scent that seemed to cling to her. Dropping to the edge of the bed, he silently cursed the fatigue that was his constant companion these days.

Zoey Kincade was not at all what he'd been expecting. He'd assumed that a woman in her profession would be a dowdy, matronly sort. He'd expected an older woman in a shapeless blue dress, her white hair twisted into a proper bun at her nape. That was the kind of woman who had cared for Barrett and his siblings. Proper English nannies.

There was nothing proper about Miss Kincade.

Closing his eyes, his mind produced an instant, vivid image of the petite woman. He couldn't help wondering what it would feel like to run his fingers through her mane of wild blond hair. That thought had occurred to him the moment he'd looked into her clear blue eyes. Yes, he decided as he pressed his forefingers against his throbbing temples, this woman was quite interesting. Her youthful features were contrasted by the quiet wisdom of her eyes. He liked her smile, as well. It had an electric effect, bathing her face in warm, welcoming light. Despite the events of the morning, he felt certain his daughter had been well cared for during his recovery.

"Poor Rachel," he muttered as he rolled his head from side to side. He was comforted by the belief that his daughter was too young for the horrible events of the past weeks to have any lasting effect. He was sure that Rachel would come out of this unscathed, but Barrett was fairly certain that the past would color the remainder of his days.

He was still a bit shaky on some of the details, but he had to content himself with the bits and pieces of memory that had survived the crash and the subsequent surgeries. For now, he was left to wonder why his wife had tried so diligently to kill him. "She must have truly hated me." Barrett sighed as he pulled the tie to his robe.

Spending these weeks in the hospital had provided him with a great deal of time in which to ponder his life. When he was released and he and Rachel were together, he vowed silently to make some major changes. That thought reminded him of something Miss Kincade had said. She had been a teacher. He wondered what event had compelled her to give up teaching to care for the children of strangers.

"Perhaps she simply loves children," he mused aloud as he waited for her to return.

That thought made him frown. It made him feel self-conscious and somehow guilty. In all his thirty-five years, he'd never given so much as a thought to the plight of other people's children. Of course, he'd never believed he'd be responsible for a child of his own, either.

"I CAN'T BELIEVE I did that," Zoey said as she walked toward the nurses huddled around Rachel.

"Did what?" one of the nurses asked.

Gently, she placed Alex into the first compartment of the double stroller. The result was predictable; he began wailing almost immediately. "Hush, baby," she pleaded. "I'll be right back as soon as I take Rachel to see her daddy."

"Rachel?" the nurse said.

Zoey nodded as she tried to coax Alex into accepting a pacifier. "I took the man the wrong baby."

"Oops," the woman said with a smile. "I'll bet he was miffed. He might be gorgeous, but he sure is a demanding guy."

"I got a small dose of that." She sighed. *Demanding* wasn't the word she would have chosen. No, she found the man reprehensible. Totally unconcerned when it came to his beautiful baby. Poor Rachel, she thought. "I can't believe I did something so stupid."

"Hey," the nurse holding Rachel chimed in. "They look so much alike, I'm surprised you can keep them straight."

Zoey smiled appreciatively. "Alex is the one who's usually crying."

"Not anymore," the nurse who had lifted him out of the stroller said.

"He's being held," Zoey said. "He calms down when he's being held."

"No wonder that woman was asking about Rachel."

Zoey was reaching for the baby when the nurse's statement stopped her cold. "What woman?"

"A tall one, a nurse."

"And she was asking about Rachel?" Zoey asked as she took the baby into her arms.

"We didn't realize this was Rachel. We told her the baby was in with her father. We said she could wait in the lounge, but I guess she was in a hurry to get back to her floor."

"Her floor?"

"She had a Radiology I.D."

Zoey was still shaking her head as she made her way back toward Barrett's room. "Who would be looking for you?" she asked the serene child. Rachel's eyelids fluttered at the sound of her voice. "Did you make a friend here when you were with Lynn and Steve?"

That was the only possible explanation, she decided. Somehow, news of their arrival must have traveled through the hospital. Rachel had been in the hospital before, after Steve and Lynn had discovered the baby abandoned.

Uneasiness quickened her pace. She paused only long enough to tap lightly on the door before pushing it open with her foot.

"Are you all right?" she asked when she saw he had moved to the bed. "Do you want me to get the nurse, Lord Montgomery?"

"No," he answered. "And please call me Rhett."

"As in Butler?" Zoey brought the baby to where he was seated on the edge of the bed. He didn't react appropriately, she thought. No warm smile, no fatherly reaction at all. In fact, he almost disregarded his daughter to respond to Zoey's question.

"My brother Herbert's doing, I'm afraid. I believe he felt it rather amusing. Herbert enjoys annoying me, always has."

"Well, if you don't mind, I think I'll stick with Barrett. It suits you. Here, this time I brought the right one."

Zoey carefully passed the baby to Barrett's outstretched arms. The transformation in the baby was incredible.

"What's wrong?" he asked, his face crumbling as he strained to be heard above Rachel's pitiful cries.

"I don't know," Zoey told him. "She never does this."

Instinctively, she reached down and scooped the baby back into her arms. Rachel stopped crying immediately. "What was that all about?" she asked in a soft voice. She checked the baby's diaper and brushed her lips against the infant's forehead.

"Is she ill?"

"She's fine," she promised him, hoping to relieve some of the panic she read in his expression. His apparent concern gave her cause to hope. Perhaps he could learn to be a caring father. "Let's try again."

They made another attempt, but Barrett was forced to content himself with touching his daughter while she was cradled in Zoey's arms. Her heart went out to the man. It was obvious that he was troubled by the baby's reaction. It was also obvious that he had no earthly idea how to relate to a baby. His self-assurance seemed to dwindle as he silently endured the child's rejection. It troubled him. That much was evident in the hesitant way he stroked her cheek, wiping away the tiny tear tracks.

"I'm sure it's just a fluke," she told him. "Rachel's a very adaptable child."

"It would appear I fared much better with Alex," Barrett said. "Rachel seems quite taken with you."

"We're pals."

"I believe you're more than that," he said as he returned to his seat on the edge of the bed. "Sorry. I don't quite have my strength up to snuff."

"You will," she assured him. "And trust me, you'll need it."

"That reality is just beginning to dawn."

She glanced over and saw the frustration causing small lines at the corners of his eyes and mouth. "What?"

"I'm being released the day after tomorrow."

"That's wonderful," Zoey said. The information hit her like a rock. Her stomach tightened at the mere thought of handing Rachel over. It was part of the job, but she never dreamed it would be so difficult. How had she become so attached to this baby in such a short time?

"Rachel is obviously very comfortable with you."

"She's a sweet baby."

"Are you genuinely fond of her?"

She gaped at him. "Of course I am."

"My home in Potomac is rather large."

"Rachel will love it, I'm sure. She likes to be on a blanket on the floor. I'm afraid my apartment has been a bit cramped. Babies require a lot of junk."

"Why don't you relocate, if you're cramped?"

She didn't want to admit that she was living off her savings and that she couldn't afford anything more extravagant than the one-bedroom apartment in Bethesda. She'd already appeared incompetent by bringing Alex to him instead of Rachel, she wasn't going to give him any more reason to think poorly of her.

"Having the two babies was unexpected," she hedged.

"I can imagine."

He bought it, she thought, as she kept her eyes averted.

"I have wall-to-wall baby stuff in the apartment. It's something of an adventure to get into the kitchen."

"Perhaps we can help each other."

Her head whipped up and she met his stare. "Help each other what?"

"I need help with Rachel. She is obviously quite taken with—"

"Lord Montgomery," she interrupted. "If you're thinking of offering me a job, thank you, but no. I have a job and I have Alex and I—"

"I was just thinking of my daughter. I apologize. Of course, you have other commitments."

"I'm sure you can find a competent nanny. I'll see if I can get some recommendations for you."

He nodded as his finger traced the baby's jawline. "I would be appreciative, Zoey. Rachel has had so many upheavals in her short life. I would very much like to get her on a more organized and regimented schedule.''

"I'm sure you'll do fine." Zoey wanted to tell him that babies didn't need a regimen as much as they needed love. This man impressed her as totally incapable of giving love. He was too staid, too proper, too distant. He was also one of the most attractive men she had ever encountered. It made absolutely no sense. Here she was, basically disgusted by his lack of any perceptible parental emotions and all she could do was fantasize about what it might be like to kiss the straight seam of his lips. The man had her thinking all sorts of wicked things. It was, she decided, sheer lunacy. Lack of sleep had obviously dulled her brain. That was the only possible explanation for her wandering thoughts.

Zoey and Barrett tried one last time to convince Rachel to go to her father. When things appeared to be getting worse rather than better, they abandoned that plan. Barrett was forced to settle for an hour-long visit of looking and very little touching.

When their time was up, Zoey held Rachel out so that he could place a kiss on her cheek. Instead of kissing his child, he simply brushed his hand over her head.

Zoey was distracted on the way home. She would miss Rachel dearly, so much so that she actually found herself considering Barrett's absurd offer to move into his big house and help him with the baby. She didn't want this sweet little girl being raised in a home devoid of love. That was how Barrett struck her, as more robot than man. The thought of sweet Rachel being raised by His Lordship was painful. And didn't the British royals customarily send their children to boarding school at the ripe old age of four or five? She shuddered and realized now what had motivated the Keatons to ask Barrett if he would relinquish his parental rights so they could adopt the little girl. Apparently, the first foster family had seen Barrett's aloofness, as well.

Susan Turner was waiting for her when she pulled into the parking spot in front of her ground-floor apartment. They had been friends since grade school. Susan was, unfortunately, a rarity. She was a wife and stay-at-home mother by choice. Zoey was continually impressed and occasionally envious of her friend's domesticity. Watching Susan in action—baking or cooking, crafting or decorating—was like watching a slice of life that was rapidly disappearing. Susan managed to do it all, even with the cloud of her husband's profession hanging over her. As much as Zoey looked forward to having a husband and family of her own, she was fairly sure she could never handle being a cop's wife.

"You look like hell."

"Thanks," Zoey grunted.

Without being asked, Susan went around to the passenger's side of the car and took the sleeping Alex out of his restraint, while Zoey took care of Rachel and the fifty-pound diaper bag. Soundlessly, they entered the apartment and managed to place each of the babies in their cribs without awakening them.

Zoey pulled the door to the bedroom closed and let out a sigh of relief. "Coffee," she said eagerly.

"Rough night?" Susan asked as she sat at the small round table adjacent to the even smaller rectangular kitchen.

"The usual," she answered as she filled the pot with water and set the basketful of grounds in place. "And I screwed up at the hospital, big-time."

Susan's green eyes sparkled. "You told the rich snob what you thought of him placing his kid in foster care?"

Shaking her head, Zoey admitted that she hadn't bothered, then explained the confusion with the babies. "The man must think I'm totally inept. He really *bothered* me. It was like he was more interested in me than in Rachel. But it doesn't matter. He'll be taking Rachel the day after tomorrow."

Susan toyed with the fringed ends of her boyishly short hair. "How are you going to handle that?"

Pulling down two mugs from the shelf, Zoey frowned. "I guess it will be fine. I mean, this is how it's supposed to happen. It's just that . . ."

"That what?"

"Rachel hated him. She cried every time the man touched her. He's about as loving and fatherly as dryer lint."

"That's weird. I thought the guy wanted to see his kid."

"Want to know something even more weird?"

Susan nodded as she tucked one tanned leg beneath her. "Sure."

"He asked me to live with him. He didn't seem to give a hoot about his daughter. He was really into finding someone to take care of her. And the leech didn't waste much time checking me out. I mean, he kept looking at me, but hardly even glanced at Rachel."

"He's quick, isn't he?"

"He's strange," Zoey insisted. "What kind of man asks you to move in with him fifteen minutes after being introduced?"

Susan frowned, her pretty features revealing her disgust. "I hate people like that. And does the guy ever plan to raise his own kid? Why do people have children if they can't be bothered—"

"We're forgetting something," Zoey interrupted. "The man's wife tried to kill him. I guess we shouldn't indict him for something that wasn't his fault. The fact that he has been absent from Rachel's life up to now really *isn't* his fault. I'm more concerned about what will happen to her when she goes to live with such a stoic, unfeeling person."

Susan pouted, apparently unwilling to give up on an issue about which she felt passionately. Zoey knew that part of her friend's passions came from being "the mother." Susan often cared for her working neighbors' children. Though she would begrudgingly acknowledge that those mothers worked out of necessity, Susan couldn't understand why every woman didn't derive pleasure from making macaroni maps and having their children's Halloween costumes sewn and pressed before Labor Day.

"So, is he going to dump Rachel on a baby-sitter?"

"He doesn't look good," Zoey explained. "Apparently, he's still weak from his injuries."

"What does an English lord look like, anyway?" Susan asked.

"Like heaven on earth," Zoey answered, then felt a blush warm her cheeks.

Susan's expression brightened. "Do tell."

"He's attractive," Zoey said. Her mind flashed a vivid image of the striking man. The mere memory of Barrett was enough to quicken her pulse.

"My new suit is attractive. I want details. Remember, I've been married forever. I have to live vicariously through you."

"You love Lou and you know it." Joining her friend at the table, Zoey locked her fingers together and allowed a small smile to pull at the corners of her mouth. "Barrett is beautiful," she admitted with a wide grin. "He's tall, dark and—"

"Deadly?" Susan finished.

Zoey's eyebrows drew together. "Meaning?"

"You were going to say, tall, dark and handsome. That usually means a man you want to look at but don't want to be involved with."

Scoffing, Zoey rose and poured two cups of coffee. Passing Susan hers, she said, "I'm hardly involved with the man."

"Do you want to be?"

"This is a ridiculous conversation. As soon as I turn Rachel over to him, we'll never cross paths again. Lord Montgomery and I don't exactly travel in the same social circles. Though I wouldn't mind needling him about that. He's so stiff."

"If you married him, would you be in line for the British throne?"

"Susan!" Zoey sloshed her coffee when she slapped her palm down on the table, laughing at the absurdity of the question. "Don't you think—"

She was interrupted by the sudden ringing of the phone. Not wanting to disturb the babies, she jumped from her seat and grabbed it on the second ring.

"Hello?"

"Miss Kincade?" a raspy, unidentifiable voice asked.

"Yes?"

"I can't let you get away with this. You'll have to be punished."

Chapter Three

After slamming the receiver onto the cradle, Zoey noted the tremor in her hand.

"Another one?" Susan asked.

She nodded. Returning to her seat, she wrapped her hands around the warm coffee mug in an attempt to ward off the chilling effect of the call.

Susan reached across the table and gave her a comforting pat on the shoulder. "Did you recognize the voice this time?"

"No. But it was exactly like the others."

"Do you want me to call Lou?"

Forcing a wan smile to her lips, she said, "No. Your husband has better things to do than to investigate my crank phone calls."

Susan's eyebrows arched high on her forehead. "This has been going on for weeks, Zoey. I think you need to consider asking for help."

"Lou already said there wasn't much anyone could do."

"What about the babies, though?"

Zoey took in a deep breath, then let it out slowly. She met her friend's concerned eyes. "You don't think me and the babies are actually in danger, do you? People get crank calls every day. It's probably just some teenager getting his jollies."

Zoey was repeating that sentiment later that evening as she prepared Alex for bed. The little boy was tired from his bath, and it seemed as if Zoey might actually be treated to a decent night's sleep.

She sat in the rocking chair, which was wedged between the two cribs. Her bed had been transformed into a twin-size changing table and makeshift dresser. As for herself, she had taken to sleeping on the couch in the living room.

Alex smelled of powder and his small body was warm and soft. She rocked him quietly until his eyelids fluttered closed.

It was just before ten o'clock when she emerged from the bedroom and tiptoed into the kitchen. She began the task of washing bottles and mixing formula, no small chore since each baby went through almost ten bottles in any twenty-four-hour period.

Because of the noise made by the wooden spoon tapping against the side of the pitcher as she stirred the formula, she almost missed the thumping sound.

Going instantly still, she held her breath and listened intently. There was the ticking of the clock above the stove, the whine of the air conditioner and then an unmistakable creak coming from the bedroom.

Dropping the pitcher of half-mixed formula into the sink, she hurried to the bedroom and shoved the door open. It took less than a second for her eyes to fix on the open window. It took only slightly longer for the figure framed in the window to react.

Zoey let out a scream as she felt along the wall for the switch. The room filled with light and the intruder jumped from the window at the same instant that Alex and Rachel responded to being jarred from their sleep. The babies cried in chorus as Zoey went to the window and shoved it closed. The chipped metal lock had been bent out of shape. She smelled fear and felt a tightness in her throat as she tried to think of what to do. The lock was broken and she was alone with two infants. What if the intruder came back? The possibility had her shaking all over.

She crawled across the bed and grabbed the telephone, pressing the emergency number with violently trembling hands.

The 9-1-1 operator was kind and she managed to calm some of Zoey's fears. As she darted her gaze around the apartment, she tried to listen for strange sounds, but the crying babies made that nearly impossible. Frantic, she clutched the telephone and was glad the operator remained on the line until the patrol car arrived.

Zoey carried Alex and Rachel into the living room and left them on a blanket on the floor while she opened the door for the two uniformed officers. "Thank you for getting here so fast," she said as she bent down to pick up Alex. For the time being, Rachel appeared to be content on the blanket. Alex quieted as soon as she lifted him onto her shoulder.

"He tried to break in through the bedroom," she explained, pointing at the now-closed door.

"Stay here," the officer whose name badge read Stevenson instructed as he and a policeman named Fulton went to check it out.

Zoey swayed with the baby in her arms, still fighting the lingering effects of the break-in. She stood over Rachel, fearful that the intruder would return. Through the opened door, she watched as the patrolman went to the window, then checked the closet and under the bed before returning to the window.

Officer Stevenson remained behind while the other man left the apartment to check what he referred to as the perimeter.

"Did you get a good look at the person?"

"No. He was tall. That's all I saw. It happened so fast. I was more worried about the babies."

"Twins?" he asked.

"No." She explained about her two charges. Then she provided the officer with what little detail she could remember about the intruder. Officer Stevenson took copious notes, but his expression remained bland.

"Is there any possibility that the break-in could be related to the babies?"

"I doubt it," Zoey answered. "Their parents are hospitalized."

"Have you noticed anyone hanging around? Maybe someone approached you in the parking lot?"

She shook her head. "The only weird thing has been the phone calls."

The officer made more notes when she told him about the weeks of crank phone calls. Officer Fulton returned and Zoey was relieved when she saw that Lou Turner, Susan's husband, had followed the patrolman through the door.

Lou was a big burly man who hardly needed the gold shield to identify him as a police detective. Lou simply looked like a cop.

"Is everyone okay?" he asked as he placed his bearlike hand on her shoulder.

"We're fine," she answered truthfully. "I might even stop shaking soon."

Lou offered a gruff smile before taking the two officers off to the corner of the room, where they formed a tight huddle. Zoey placed the now-sleeping Alex on the sofa, bracing his small body with a pile of cushions. She did the same with Rachel, making sure both babies were safe before she pulled the afghan down to cover them.

"They found a set of footprints outside the window," Lou said as he and the other officers came to stand with her.

"The lock on the window is broken," she said.

"I know. You can get it fixed tomorrow. I'm going to take you and the kids back to our house tonight."

Zoey nodded. "Thanks."

"These two officers will remain here to meet the lab people."

"Lab people?"

"We have to process the crime scene."

Zoey closed her eyes and fought against the tears that threatened. It was unnerving hearing her home referred to as a crime scene.

"WHAT ARE YOU going to do?" Susan asked as soon as her two young sons had scrambled out of the kitchen.

"I'm going to take up Lord Montgomery on his offer."

"Excuse me?"

Zoey kept her eyes on Rachel, who was lying across her knees, holding a finger in each tiny fist. "I'm afraid to go back to my apartment. I'm tired of getting those calls. If you don't mind helping me get these guys in the car, I'd like to go back to the hospital to see if His Lordship's offer is still open."

"Have you lost your mind?" Susan asked. "You don't know anything about that man. He could be a serial killer, for all you know."

"The man is some sort of minor royalty," Zoey countered.

"Which should make you even more cautious. Come on. There's so much inbreeding in the royal family, who knows what kind of madness can result in a man whose family tree doesn't fork."

Zoey sighed.

"You're welcome to stay here," Susan offered.

Zoey smiled at her friend's kind but impractical suggestion. "Thanks, but I don't think it would be fair to Lou and the boys if I moved in. I come with two babies in tow, remember?"

"We can manage."

"There's no need to," Zoey insisted as she shifted Rachel and stood up. "All I need is a change of location just long enough to have my window and my nerves fixed. A few weeks in some luxury digs off River Road sounds perfect, don't you think?"

"I think you're opening a can of worms."

"Susan, *what* is that supposed to mean?"

Her friend dried her hands on the towel hanging off the handle of the heavily decorated refrigerator. "I just think going to live under the roof of some man you don't know is crazy."

"Social Services did a routine background check. Barrett Montgomery lives like a hermit. He doesn't have any bad habits—"

"That they know about."

Determined, Zoey raised the strap of her purse over her head and claimed the diaper bag. "I'm going to go check things out. He may tell me to forget it when he realizes that Alex is coming along for the ride."

Zoey's convictions didn't waiver on the trip to the hospital. If anything, her resolve was stronger by the time she and Rachel appeared at the nurses' station.

"Miss Kincade?" the duty nurse inquired, obviously surprised to see Zoey and the babies. "I didn't realize that you had made arrangements for another visit."

"I haven't," she admitted. "But Rachel had a difficult night last night and I can only assume it was because she missed her daddy."

The nurse grinned at Zoey's fib and gave her a nod of approval.

Zoey silently apologized to Rachel for involving her in a lie, but she needed to get in to see the lord and the small falsehood seemed the most judicious route.

SHE WAS EVEN more beautiful. That was his first thought when she appeared in the doorway holding his daughter.

"So, whose child have you brought me today?" he teased, enjoying the slight pink hue that colored her high cheekbones. He shifted in the hospital bed.

"Sorry, no surprises today."

Rachel was dressed in a plain pink jumper, and he was amazed to see that the baby's eyes were wide open when Zoey handed her to him. No sooner had Zoey slipped her hand away from the baby than Rachel began to cry. He tried holding her more tightly. He tried holding her against his chest. He tried rocking her gently in his arms. Nothing seemed to appease the baby. Nothing except being handed back to Zoey. He was so frazzled by the child's reaction that he couldn't pass her to Zoey fast enough.

"I don't know what her problem is," Zoey said as she looked nervously back and forth between him and the infant.

"It is rather disheartening," he admitted.

"I'm sure she'll be fine once the two of you are back home together."

She astounded him by sitting on the edge of his bed.

Gravity was kind enough to pull him toward her, allowing his leg to brush the side of her slender hip. She was dressed much the same as on the previous day, in a long, flowing dress obviously selected because it attempted to obliterate the outline of her body. If her motivation for wearing the garment was to keep men from noticing her curves, she'd missed the mark. Indeed, he was intrigued. His mind conjured a guess at what she might look like under all that flowered fabric.

"Does your offer still hold?"

It took a second for his brain to switch gears. "My offer?"

"Would you still like me to help you with Rachel?"

"Yes. By all means. Certainly."

"I have a few things to tell you that might change your mind."

Fascinated, Barrett lifted his arm and placed it behind his head. He nodded his desire for her to continue and struggled to keep his eyes from staring openly at the fullness of her lips. "Do go on," he urged.

"First off, I would have to bring Alex with me."

Barrett hesitated only a second before saying, "I'm sure that won't present a problem. By now, Rachel is probably quite accustomed to having him around."

He watched as relief brightened her features. Yet, he saw something very much like reluctance clouding her pretty blue eyes.

"My apartment was broken into last night."

He felt his eyebrows pull together and the tightness where his head wound was still healing. "Are you all right?"

She nodded as she grabbed a handful of her hair and flipped it back over her shoulder. "Just scared."

"The children are both—"

"Fine," she finished.

He stroked the stubble on his chin. "And this event is what has caused you to rethink your decision to work for me?"

"No. I don't want to work for you. I will help make Rachel's transition into your care as smooth as possible. In return, I would appreciate it if we could stay with you until the police discover who has been taunting me."

"I'm afraid I don't understand. Isn't it highly unlikely that the police will discover the person responsible for breaking into your apartment? I was under the impression that that sort of random crime was difficult to resolve."

"They have footprints and some fingerprints," she explained. "They think it's the same person who has been bothering me with harassing telephone calls."

"What kind of harassing calls?"

She shrugged her delicate shoulders. The action caused his daughter to wave her small fist in apparent protest.

"Standard issue. Veiled threats."

"How long has this been going on?"

"Since about the time I got Alex. Three weeks, maybe a month."

"So, you would like to seek refuge in my home?"

"In return for helping you with Rachel."

The fact that she had approached him as a negotiator appealed to his business sense. She was definitely one interesting woman, full of surprises. Yesterday, he would have bet any amount that she would never change her mind. He could only conclude that the calls and the break-in were sufficiently alarming to have brought about this sudden change of mind.

"You have a deal, Miss Kincade. I'll expect you and the children here at ten tomorrow morning when I'm released."

THE NEXT MORNING had started early for Zoey. With Lou standing guard, she had returned to her apartment long enough to pack what she needed for herself and the babies. She had called Social Services and alerted them to her new address, conveniently leaving out the reason for the sudden move.

"Do you know what you're doing?" Lou asked as he placed the last box into the trunk of her car.

"Probably not," Zoey admitted. "How bad can it be? The guy's rich and important. He obviously needs help with basic parenting skills. While you concentrate on figuring out who's been doing all this stuff to me, I can concentrate on teaching His Lordship how to take care of Rachel."

"Assuming he wants to learn," Lou returned. "Some men just aren't cut out for fatherhood."

"It's a bit late for Lord Montgomery. He's got a child, and I'm going to make sure he turns into a nurturing, loving father."

She arrived at the hospital with the two babies at a quarter of eleven. Judging from the cool reception she received, the lord didn't care for her tardiness.

"Do you realize the time?"

Zoey forced herself to meet his unwavering stare with a bright smile. "Believe it or not, babies can't tell time. They have this magical ability to throw even the best-intentioned schedule right out the window."

"You could have called me," he said.

"Gee," Zoey said thoughtfully, "I guess I should have thought to put my cell phone in the diaper bag."

"Indeed."

She chuckled. "I was being facetious. I don't have a cell phone."

The look he offered was one of total disbelief. He stood gaping at her from across the neatly made hospital bed.

In spite of the fact that she didn't think much of him, she grudgingly acknowledged that he looked particularly good in street clothes. A pale green polo shirt outlined a well-developed upper torso that angled and tapered to a trim waist. His slacks were pleated and he looked so put together, Zoey had to remind herself that he had just spent the better part of two months in a hospital.

"I've already completed all the paperwork, so we can be on our way," he said.

"Not yet," she told him.

Zoey reached down and plucked Rachel from the stroller. Without warning, she thrust the baby at him. "You haven't properly wished your daughter a good morning."

He appeared perturbed, but Rachel seemed even more disconcerted by the unexpected contact. No sooner had Zoey removed her arm from the child's back than Rachel began to cry in earnest.

"Take her," he pleaded.

Shaking her head, she reclaimed the child, who stopped crying almost immediately. "Maybe she senses your reluctance."

"Pardon me?" he asked.

Looking up into his dark eyes, Zoey explained, "Rachel is obviously picking up on the fact that you're uncomfortable with her."

He frowned but said nothing. He lifted the strap of an expensive-looking leather overnight bag onto one broad shoulder.

"Don't we have to wait for a wheelchair?" she asked.

He scoffed. "I think I am fully capable of leaving this place of my own volition."

Too bad you aren't capable of caring for your daughter of your own volition, Zoey thought as she put Rachel in the stroller and followed him out the door.

"That's mine," she said, inclining her head in the direction of her maroon compact.

His Lordship regarded the car with what she could only describe as thinly veiled contempt. "Sorry." She sighed. "My Mercedes is in the shop."

"I see."

She laughed. "That was a joke."

He blinked at her, his dark eyebrows drawn together. "I see."

Great conversationalist, she thought as she placed Rachel in her car seat. "You can help," she suggested when she noted the man standing idly by.

"What shall I do?"

"Take Alex and put him in the car."

He placed his bag on the macadam and lifted the little boy out of his seat. Carrying him like a sack of flour, Barrett took Alex around to the opposite side of the car. Zoey remained still, totally amused as she watched him pondering his dilemma. After a brief period, he shifted Alex so that the child was tucked beneath his arm like a football. He then lifted the door handle and, after a little more rearranging, managed to get the baby into the car seat.

"There you are," he said, smiling proudly at his accomplishment.

"Not quite."

"What?"

Meeting his questioning eyes, she swallowed her grin and said, "You didn't fasten the safety belt."

"Oh," he mouthed before his head disappeared again into the back seat.

She stayed by the driver's door even when she heard his muffled curse. "You fit the—"

"I see how it works," he cut in irritably.

Yep, she thought as she slid behind the wheel, Lord Montgomery had a great deal to learn. She only hoped that she could teach him before he got too frustrated and turned Rachel over to a nanny.

"Damn," he muttered as he banged his knee against the glove compartment while trying to fit his large frame into the small import.

"Watch your language around the children," she teased.

"I doubt if I have to concern myself with being repeated at this early stage."

"It's never too early to begin developing good habits."

He sighed loudly. "Are you going to be this disagreeable on a regular basis?"

Chancing a look at him from the corner of her eye, Zoey could tell there was no real malice behind the complaint. "Consider my suggestion as part of a larger scheme," she told him. "By the time I'm finished, you'll be the best father in all Potomac."

He grunted. "Highly unlikely."

"Lack of ability or lack of interest?" she asked as she turned out of the parking lot.

"Let's get something straight," he began as he shifted uncomfortably in the seat. "I simply want what is best for Rachel. I'm not interested in becoming anything other than competent."

"Lofty aspirations," she countered. "Raising children is about—"

"Child," he corrected.

Zoey sighed. There would be plenty of time to convince him of the importance of nurturing Rachel. No need to browbeat him on his first day home.

"Zoey?" he asked.

"Yes?" She hated the way her heart fluttered when she heard her name on his lips.

"I think we'd best stop at the grocery store. I called my housekeeper, but I neglected to instruct her regarding these babies. I'm sure they must require specific items and such."

"You're catching on, Your Lordship. Is there a grocery store near your house?"

"I don't care for being referred to as Your Lordship."

"Forgive me, sire. What does one call you?"

"Barrett is fine, remember?"

"Okay, Barrett, where's the grocery store?"

After clearing his throat he said, "I believe there is one on the left-hand side just after the off-ramp."

Luckily, they were stopped at a traffic light. It afforded Zoey the opportunity to simply stare in disbelief. "You've never been to the grocery store, have you?"

The angle of his chin became more severe and defensiveness narrowed his eyes. "I have a housekeeper. She's on holiday currently, but deliveries have been seen to."

Shaking her head, Zoey said, "Living with you is going to be a real education."

"I can mirror that sentiment," Barrett said.

"Good, then we can learn from each other. Your first lesson will be a formal introduction to the baby-food aisle."

"Sounds thrilling," he grumbled.

It was Saturday, the worst possible day to go into a grocery store. "You're getting trial by fire," she told him as she took Rachel out of her car seat. "Grab Alex and welcome to purgatory."

"Purgatory?"

She smiled as the scent of fresh-baked cinnamon rolls reached her nostrils. The chore of packing and getting the babies ready for the move had prevented her from having breakfast.

"Saturday is a busy day at the store. I try to get all my shopping done during the week so I don't have to compete with the people who can only come on Saturday. You're about to learn what can happen when a harmless-looking cart is turned into a near-lethal weapon."

Surprisingly, Barrett appeared to be very interested in the ins and outs of grocery shopping. He seemed to approach it with the same interest people show when they study a different culture.

"Rule number one," she said as she selected a cart from the row outside the store. "No matter which cart you choose, you end up with one that has an off-center wheel, making it impossible to steer."

"Why is that?"

She shrugged. "Think of it as part of the ritual." Moving the cart to the side, she said, "I'm going to put Rachel in the baby seat. You can either carry Alex or push the cart. Your choice."

She watched as he stroked his chin pensively. "I believe that if I am to get the most out of this adventure, I should handle the cart."

"Deal," Zoey said, strapping Rachel in place. "Rule number two," she said as she led him toward the entrance. "Never come to the grocery store hungry."

"And why is that?"

"Because everything, even bean curd, looks appetizing."

"I like bean curd," he countered.

"Why doesn't that surprise me?" she said under her breath as they filed into the crowded store. "Stay with me," she instructed. "The key is to get in and quickly get out."

"Is that why they have that lane for ten items or less?"

Zoey snorted. "No, that lane is for people with fifteen items who are too lazy to stand in a regular line. Then they write a check without a check-cashing card."

"Am I supposed to have some sort of card?" he asked, pushing the cart alongside her.

"I use cash, so I'll be happy to cover you this time," she teased. "But only if you stay behind me. These aisles are two-way and you're taking up the whole aisle.''

"Sorry," he grumbled.

Though the bakery department was calling her, Zoey knew they should hurry. Barrett had not complained, but she noted a tiredness around his eyes and she didn't want to be responsible for the man collapsing in the middle of the produce section.

"Why are there so many varieties?" he asked when she came to a halt in front of a huge display of infant formulas.

"Babies are little people, complete with different tastes in food."

"What about all those diapers? Do babies have different types of . . . plumbing, as well?"

She laughed and for a brief instant she allowed herself to look directly into his eyes. It was a magical moment. There was something different about this man, something that seemed to stir and churn her insides. "As a matter of fact . . ." Her voice trailed off as she lowered her eyes so they fixed on the front of his shirt. It was a mistake, since she found herself staring at the dark curly hair peeking out at the top. It made her wonder if his entire chest was covered by soft, dark hair. Embarrassed by her own thoughts, she raised her eyes.

"As a matter of fact, what?"

The warmth of a blush reached her cheeks, and she was glad he couldn't see her face. "Baby boys and baby girls do require some engineering differences in their diapers. Rachel uses those and Alex uses those,'' she said, pointing to the different brands. ''We have to—'' She halted abruptly when she heard Barrett's disgusted grunt. She could feel the dampness along the shoulder of her dress and knew that Alex had outdone himself.

''What should I do?'' Barrett asked, though he made no move to come anywhere near Zoey, not when Alex was still vomiting.

''Here,'' she said as she handed him her purse. ''Get a case of that formula and one box each of the diapers. There's money in my wallet. I'll take Alex outside and clean us both up.''

''What about the floor?'' he asked, gesturing in the direction of the small puddle.

''I'll suggest they do a cleanup on my way out.''

''Wait!'' he called, grabbing her arm. ''Are you leaving me alone with Rachel?''

Shaking her head, Zoey said, ''Just leave her in the cart. If she starts to cry, try giving her a royal command to stop.''

Hurrying, she carried the soiled child out of the store, stopping only briefly to alert an employee of the mess in the baby aisle. She took in some deep breaths when she emerged from the store, trying to rid her nostrils of the foul smell. ''No benches,'' she grumbled. ''Great.'' She sat down on the warm concrete and cleaned Alex as best she could.

She pulled another cart from the row and placed Alex inside, careful to latch the safety belt securely.

Zoey pushed it to the far end of the pickup area so she wasn't in the way of the dozens of people trying to load their cars.

"Hush, baby," she said as she knelt down to search through the diaper bag. It took a few seconds for her to find the box of wipes and extract one. "Just a minute," she said as she took the cloth and began dabbing at the dampness on her shoulder.

Her eyes were watering as she pulled another cloth from the box, sat down on the concrete and yanked on her dress to be able to reach the lower portion of the stain. She was in this contorted position when the screech of car tires sounded and a flash of white caught her eye. It took a second for her to realize that the car had stopped mere inches from her and that the flash of white was actually a pair of running shoes. She looked up to see a tall woman, wearing a large, floppy hat. To her horror, Zoey realized that the woman was trying to take Alex out of his seat.

Chapter Four

Barrett found Zoey sprawled on the pavement, surrounded by a collection of people. Using the shopping cart, he created a path through the small group of strangers. Her hair was a wild mass and her eyes were large and brimming with fear. He was surprised by his reaction to seeing her look so shaken and vulnerable. The urge to kneel next to her was very strong.

"What happened?" he asked.

She looked up at him, her face pale. He could see her hand shaking as she patted Alex's back.

"Some woman tried to take the baby," she said in a strained voice.

He reached out and took her hand, gently pulling her to her feet. It was only then that he saw the reddish splotch on the side of her face. The sight caused an unfamiliar knot in his stomach. "What's that?"

"She kicked me," Zoey explained.

Her statement was punctuated by a small shiver. Barrett placed his arm across her shoulders and pulled her and the baby against his chest. He could feel her anxiety as her body trembled against his.

"Are you okay?"

Her hair was like silk where it touched his arm as she offered a silent nod. He could smell the fresh, floral scent of her hair.

"Did any of you see what happened?" he asked as he surveyed the crowd.

He received a chorus of negative responses before a tall, lanky young man dressed in the bright red uniform of the store stepped forward.

"I...uh...seen the car the lady got into."

"Did you get the license-plate number?"

He shook his head. The action caused several strands of limp brown hair to fall across his eyes. He made no move to clear his vision.

"Did you see the woman?"

As he again shook his head, Barrett felt frustration beginning to shroud his initial alarm. He struggled to keep the annoyance from his voice. "What exactly did you see?"

"The car."

"And?" Barrett prompted.

The man shifted his weight from foot to foot, then said, "It was white. A two-door. I think it was an American model."

He was about to launch into a grilling of the young man, when Zoey tugged herself out of his grasp. He felt an emptiness when she was no longer against him, a rather obscure sense of abandonment that he knew full well he shouldn't be feeling. He decided that it was nothing more than a reaction to his first real human contact in many months. His musing was interrupted by his daughter. Rachel let out a piercing cry that nearly made him jump.

"Here," Zoey said as she passed Alex to him.

Actually, she thrust the child against him, leaving him no option but to accept the infant.

"Hush," she soothed as she unfastened the seat belt and lifted Rachel out of the shopping cart's built-in infant seat.

She turned then and raised her chin, so that her face was tilted upward. Meeting his eyes, she said, "Could we just go?"

Barrett nodded. There was no way he could have refused her request. Not when he saw that she was still trembling.

"Don't you want to file a report with the police?" a man asked.

Barrett read the shiny metal name tag and realized the question had come from the store's assistant manager. He looked at Zoey, communicating the unspoken question, and receiving her unspoken response in return. Then, looking back at the manager, he said, "Give me your card and we'll contact the authorities after Miss Kincade has an opportunity to compose herself."

He held Alex in one arm and used the other to steer the cart to where she had parked her car. After assisting Zoey with the children, and placing her in the passenger's seat, he lifted the trunk and rammed the shopping bags around the suitcases and the stroller. It wasn't an easy chore. But once it was accomplished, he slipped behind the wheel.

"You can't do that."

"Do what?" he asked.

"You can't leave the cart in the middle of the road. You take it to one of those."

Following the line of her pointing finger, he saw the brightly painted railings and the huge sign that read Cart Drop-off. He wanted to tell her that the store employees could retrieve their own bloody carts, but he knew she was still upset and he had no desire to add to her distress.

Reluctantly, he got out and did her bidding. Returning to the car, he extended his hand in her direction, palm up. "The keys, please? They aren't in your purse."

The diaper bag was, apparently, another purse. She rummaged around inside the thing, which she had stuffed between her feet in the front seat. It was then that Barrett detected a sour smell.

As if reading his thoughts, Zoey said, "In all the confusion, I didn't get a chance to get myself or Alex totally cleaned up. Your shirt is probably a total loss, too."

Looking down, he noticed a decidedly unpleasant-smelling smear.

"You'll get used to it," Zoey assured him.

"I seriously doubt that." Barrett backed out of the parking lot and pointed the car in the direction of his home. "Should we seek some sort of medical attention for your injury?"

"No. But I think we should contact the police. Especially after what happened last night at my apartment."

"Do you think the person who attempted to take Alex was the same person responsible for your break-in?"

He heard her take in a deep breath and let it out slowly before saying, "No."

He digested the response for a moment then asked, "What did happen?"

"I was sitting on the ground—"

"Why?"

"I was trying to wipe the back part of my dress, and I didn't want to fall over in the process."

"Then what happened?" He gave a quick glance in her direction. There were deep furrows between her eyes and the corners of her mouth were slightly downcast.

"I heard the car stop at the curb. Then I got a glimpse of feet. When I realized the woman was trying to—"

"How do you know it was a woman?" he cut in.

"Her ankle."

"Excuse me?"

"She had thin ankles. No man could have a thin ankle like that, and there was something weird about her leg."

"Weird?"

"Yes, weird." Her voice held an edge of annoyance.

"How so?"

"I don't know. It just felt weird. Like she had some sort of textured hose on."

Barrett digested the events as he pulled into his driveway. He was momentarily distracted by seeing the place again. Though he had spent painstaking months overseeing the design and construction of the single-story residence, it now felt very much like a foreign place. Foreign and slightly sad. He couldn't look at it without thinking of Alice and violence, of madness. Alice had insisted on building a house even though he had no idea how long he would stay in America.

"It's big," Zoey said.

"I believe I told you we could all fit comfortably here."

Comfortable was an understatement, she thought as she climbed the two steps and stood in front of massive mahogany double doors. She held a baby in each arm while Barrett slipped a key into a highly polished brass lock. She remained outside while he disarmed the alarm.

When he motioned her inside, Zoey had to fight to keep her mouth from dropping open. It was like something out of a magazine. It had a definite decorator's flair. The foyer was polished wood, decorated on either side by antique pieces and ornately framed artwork. The small oval rug in muted shades looked too expensive to dare walk on. Barrett marched forward, apparently immune to the surroundings. Not Zoey. She was impressed by the beautiful rugs, tapestries and upholstered pieces. It was as if he had replicated a formal English home smack-dab in the center of Montgomery County.

"Rachel's room is this way," he called as he glanced back at her. "We should take care of Alex before we start on anything else."

Zoey smiled. "Get used to it," she warned.

"I don't believe that is possible."

"This is really cute," Zoey said as she reached the beautifully appointed room. It was the perfect girl's room, pink and frilly with state-of-the-art baby-care equipment.

"My wife spared no expense. You should find everything you need."

His words were strained, and he left the room almost immediately after mentioning his deceased wife. Carefully, Zoey placed Rachel in the small bassinet in the corner, then she took Alex over to the changing table. Barrett's tone had given away nothing of his feelings, though Zoey wondered if it was humanly possible to have feelings for a woman who had tried to murder you on not one, but two occasions. "Stranger things have happened," she told Alex as she peeled the soiled clothing away from his tiny body. It took her some time, but when she was finished, Alex smelled like soap and baby powder. Even more amazing was that both Rachel and Alex had fallen asleep, Rachel in the bassinet and Alex in the frilly pink-and-white crib.

Zoey flipped on the baby monitor and soundlessly backed out of the room, and ran right into something solid. She almost screamed out, thanks to the lingering effects of the past twenty-four hours. But the hand that appeared at her elbow, the hand steadying her, was somehow familiar. As was the firm outline of muscle pressing against her back.

"Careful," Barrett said.

The word he spoke was soft, barely whispered. She could feel his breath in her hair, warming her ear and producing a slight tingle in the pit of her stomach. That odd feeling forced her to consider vaulting away from him.

"Sorry," she mumbled.

"I'll show you to your room," he said. The deep, almost seductive whisper was gone, replaced by an efficient, clipped tone.

"If you're in the middle of something..."

He peered at her, the corner of his mouth twitching slightly. "I do believe we would both be happier if you had an opportunity to...freshen up."

Zoey felt her face redden. She'd almost forgotten that she had been the one holding Alex in the grocery store. "You're right. Please."

Barrett led her past three closed doors before he stopped in front of one and turned the knob. The room was huge. A bed that looked more like a regal platform stood to the right. Her suitcase had been placed at the foot of the carved four-poster. No fewer than three dressers occupied various walls. As she entered, she saw a long, narrow closet filled with clothing. Women's clothing.

She looked up and met Barrett's dark eyes questioningly.

"I'll have Rosita remove the clothing on Monday."

Zoey didn't look away and neither did he. They seemed to be locked in a kind of silent communication. Zoey didn't dare ask the question foremost in her mind and Barrett didn't appear ready to offer additional information.

"Thanks," Zoey mumbled. He'd won the battle; she'd blinked first.

"I'll put on some tea. Would you care for some?"

She shook her head. "I don't do tea. I'm a coffee person."

"I see. The bath is through there. I believe you'll find everything satisfactory."

After he'd left, she stared at the closed door. "I think I made a huge mistake," she whispered. She hadn't given much thought to the fact that the man had only recently lost his wife. Frowning, she went to the bed and flipped the locks on her suitcase. Lifting her carefully folded dresses, she went to the closet.

Unable to resist, she reached out and stuck her hand beneath a plastic sleeve and fingered the tailored suit beneath. It was like something Jacqueline Kennedy would have worn. It was simple, elegant and looked as if it had never been taken out of its packaging. "Lady Montgomery had great taste," she said with a sigh. As she hung her clothes on the rod, it became instantly apparent that she had entered a different world. Even the hangers she had brought from home were outclassed by the fancy fabric-covered ones evenly spaced along the bar. Zoey turned slowly in the closet, making a mental tally of the contents. She guessed there were easily fifty suits, dresses and gowns and an equal number of shoes. The top shelves were loaded with hatboxes, purses and monogrammed sweater bags. It boggled the mind.

The bathroom was equally impressive. The tub could easily accommodate two, which made Zoey wonder. She tried to imagine staid Barrett frolicking in the deep, marble tub. The image was somehow disturbing. It wasn't that she didn't want to think of him having a good time. For some reason, she just didn't like the idea of Barrett in such an intimate setting.

"Stop it," she warned herself. "I must be sleep-deprived or something. Why else am I thinking these ridiculous thoughts?"

Zoey chased them away by stepping beneath the steaming stream from the shower head. She found a selection of robes on a hook in the dressing area adjacent to the shower. They were the same posh velour as the robe Barrett had been wearing that first day at the hospital. The garment was amazingly heavy. So much so that she hurried into her slip and her dress, leaving her feet bare. Twisting her hair into a braid, she checked her face in the mirror. A purple bruise was beginning to form at the top of her cheekbone.

"No need for makeup," she muttered. "I've already got enough color on my face."

Barrett was waiting for her when she came down the hall. He called her name and she followed the sound. Bypassing the elegant living room, she moved down a corridor toward his voice.

Barrett was perched on a stool at the counter facing into a kitchen long enough to qualify as a galleyway. His eyes seemed to blaze a slow path over her face, all the way down to her feet. His expression didn't relay any particular emotion. His lack of reaction was something of an affront to her femininity.

She forced her gaze to another area of the room. Appliances were polished to a high sheen. Beyond her host she could see a large room with a stunning slate fireplace and elegantly casual furniture. It was the only part of the house she'd seen so far that didn't remind her of a museum.

"I smell coffee."

He smiled. It wasn't a real smile but more of an almost imperceptible curl of his mouth. Zoey knew that had she not been looking at him, she surely would have missed the subtle action.

"Too bad you Americans never learned to appreciate fine English tea."

"Fine English tea is a contradiction in terms," she quipped. "Where do you keep the cups?"

"I don't believe I should tell you. Not until you apologize for that treasonous remark."

Zoey shrugged her shoulders and started opening cabinets. She got lucky on the third try. Pouring a cup from the designer coffee machine capable of brewing everything from run-of-the-mill to flavored lattés, she moved around and joined him at the counter.

"I see you've changed," she said with an appreciative nod. The man certainly knew how to dress. He had that kind of understated style that allowed him to look positively dashing in a pair of chinos and a plaid shirt. "Nice tassels."

"Tassels?"

"Your shoes."

"You don't like my shoes?"

"They're fine," she said, lifting her cup to her lips. She almost laughed as she watched him frown and examine his footwear.

"These are quite comfortable."

"I'm sure."

"The craftsmanship is sound."

"No doubt."

"Then what is it you don't like?"

She sighed and said, "I like them."

"No, you don't."

"Fine. I don't."

"I knew it. What do you have against my shoes?"

"I don't have anything against your shoes. It's just that they..."

"They what?"

"Never mind."

"Zoey, please tell me."

"I think the tassels are dorky."

"Dorky?"

"You know. Silly, stupid, rid—"

"I am aware of the meaning of dorky."

His shoulders stiffened slightly and he raised his chin. "I happen to like tassels. I like them more than, let's say, loud floral prints."

Zoey looked down at her dress, then glared at him. "You're only criticizing my dress because I made fun of your shoes."

He shook his head, then took a sip of tea. "No, I'm not. That would be childish, don't you agree?"

There was an amused twinkle in his eyes that belied his remark. She wasn't going to argue fashion with the man. What was the point? Still, she couldn't deny that she had enjoyed sparring with him. It made him seem more real, more approachable. She needed to get to know him. It was the only way she could find out the best way to reach him. The best way to help him learn to raise his daughter.

"You really should put something on your cheek. Ice, perhaps?" he suggested.

She agreed. "Good idea, if I want to keep the swelling down."

Barrett rose, opened a drawer and grabbed a plastic bag. After filling it with ice, he wrapped it in a kitchen towel and handed it to her. Their fingers touched for a brief moment. The contact was limited but the effect lingered. Her hand tingled where they had touched, and her stomach contracted in an odd tightness that managed to alter her breathing slightly.

"How did you get the bruise?"

"I told you, she kicked me."

"You never intimated it was so violent."

"I guess she was so determined to get away that her heel got to visit with my cheek."

"Did it hurt?"

She chuckled. "It sure did. I think the last time I was hit in the face was when I was six years old and wouldn't give Jerry Rivers the ball."

"Rather aggressive of the boy to hit you because of it, don't you think?"

"Not really," she admitted. "It was his ball and I was teasing him, holding it over his head. He was only four, so I don't think we should be too hard on him."

"Good point." Barrett took another sip of his tea. "We should contact the authorities."

Zoey nodded. "I have a friend who's a cop. I'll call Lou later."

"I'd rather you keep some ice on this first," he said, indicating her bruised cheek. He sat next to her.

Apparently, he intended to help her with the ice pack. He covered her hand with his, lacing his large fingers with hers. His hand was warm, smooth and much bigger than her own. It was a harmless action; he was simply trying to assist in case her arm became tired from holding it in place. Barrett had no idea what the innocent gesture was doing to her insides, especially her ability to concentrate.

Finally, his touch became more of a distraction than a help, and she stepped away from him. At about the same time, one of the babies began to cry.

"That's our call," she said, then grinned mischievously at Barrett. "Now's your chance. If you thought the grocery store was fun, you'll *love* this."

"What do we do?" Barrett asked.

"Did you bring in the stuff from the store?" she asked. When he indicated that he had, she said, "You go get whoever is crying and I'll make up some bottles."

She found the formula and the packages of diapers near the front door. She was in the process of searching for something to mix the formula in, when Barrett reappeared, carrying Alex.

At first glance, she knew that something was amiss, but it wasn't clear until Barrett shifted the baby in his arms and snagged his shirt.

"*Staples*, Barrett?" she groaned.

Defensively, he answered, "I changed his diaper."

"Let me see," she demanded, lifting the child away from him. "I don't believe this."

"I should think you would thank me."

"I can't believe you did this." She moved around the counter and placed the baby on the floor. Alex immediately began crying. "Hold your hand against his skin while I tear this. Then you can go get another diaper."

"I had to use staples," he retorted. "I didn't have any glue in my office."

"The diapers come with adhesive tapes," she explained. "See? You fold these back. You do not staple or use other sharp objects. Understand?"

He was about to respond, when the sound of Rachel's cries echoed down the hall.

"Make that two diapers," she corrected. "You'll have to keep them happy while I mix formula."

Zoey moved as fast as she could, but it wasn't fast enough for her two charges. Barrett tried to calm Rachel, but the baby girl wanted nothing to do with him. He fared better with Alex, who quieted when Barrett held him. The five minutes it took to fix the bottles felt like an eternity to Zoey, so she knew it had to be worse on Barrett since he wasn't accustomed to the demands of two hungry infants.

"Here," she said as she passed him a bottle. Then she gathered Rachel and went into the family room. It wasn't until she was seated in an overstuffed chair that she realized Barrett was still standing in the kitchen. "It's easier if you sit down," she explained. Balancing the bottle in the baby's mouth with her chin, she got two clean cloth diapers out of the bag. "Put this under his chin while he's eating and on your shoulder when you burp him."

"Burp him?" Barrett repeated, as if she had just asked him to perform delicate brain surgery.

"Follow along with me," she instructed.

Once Barrett got the rhythm of it, he was fine. In fact, there was a point near the end when Zoey thought he might actually be enjoying himself. Until, of course, Alex vomited most of his bottle all over Barrett and the chair he'd been sitting in. To his credit, Barrett hadn't pitched the baby onto the floor, though there was a second there when Zoey thought he might do just that.

"Put him on the blanket on the floor for now," she told him. "I'll take care of him after I finish feeding Rachel."

"Thank you."

HE STOPPED at the entranceway to the kitchen and dragged in a deep ragged breath. He silently reproached himself for all but abandoning the woman with the two fretful infants. He'd stayed in his room long after his shower, hiding like a coward. He fixed his gaze on her body, or rather her backside. She was on her knees in front of the soiled chair, furiously scrubbing away the stain. Folding his arms across his chest, he leaned against the wall, content just to study her from the safe distance.

The pastel shades of the summer sky reflected off her now-dry hair. She had taken it out of that silly braid so that it fell well below her shoulders. It reminded him of a field of shimmering wheat. Her body inspired no such pastoral ideas. No, when he looked at her, he felt the unmistakable stirrings of lust. It wasn't something he would act upon. His upbringing insured that he would comport himself in an appropriate fashion. But he could certainly fantasize.

Her dress was twisted and pulled tight, allowing him to see the true outline of her figure. She was thin, but not in an anorexic way. No, this lady had womanly curves and beautiful legs. He sighed his appreciation.

Unfortunately, he sighed loudly enough so that Zoey spun around. It made him feel guilty when he saw the remnants of fear in her eyes.

"Just me," he said.

She visibly relaxed and offered him a smile that he felt all the way to his feet.

"I thought you had gone to bed," she said as she rose. "Did I make too much noise filling the bucket?"

He shook his head, only then noticing the pail by her foot. "Sorry that I left you in the middle of feeding the babies. Are they asleep?"

"Yep." She waved her dainty hand in his direction. "Sorry Alex barfed on you. I'll feed him from now on, if you like, but I won't guarantee you'll be totally safe."

He watched as she went to the counter, emptied the water into the sink, then rinsed the bucket, and finally her hands.

"Rosita could have taken care of that—"

"Trust me," she interrupted. "You don't want to leave that stuff sitting too long."

"I see your point."

"I made some pasta. Sit down and I'll get you some."

"I don't expect you to cook for me."

"Good," she answered. "It's always nice to do things for people who don't expect it. They tend to appreciate the effort. Now, sit."

"Yes, ma'am."

When she had the plate in the microwave, he remarked, "I am impressed. I've been in this house for three years and I never have been able to master that contraption."

"The miracle of the Time Cook button," she teased. "My college education pays dividends daily."

"You mentioned you were a teacher?" he asked. It felt good to have someone to talk to. He had a pretty good idea of what her duties would be here, but he wanted to talk. All those weeks in the hospital had left him hungry for conversation. That was the only possible explanation for such a ridiculous opening line. He must simply be starved for human contact.

"Was," she corrected. "And I should be able to stay out for a year, if I stick to my budget."

"Budget?"

"Yeah," she said as she placed the plate of food in front of him.

The pesto smelled wonderful. He took a deep breath, savoring his first real food in what felt like years.

"A budget is what people like me live on and people like you design."

Crooking one eyebrow, he asked, "Is that a criticism?"

"More like envy," she said, pulling the cork from a bottle of wine and filling his glass. "I hope you don't mind. I got this out of that room behind the pantry. You have more wine stored in there than my corner store stocks. I have no idea if this is the right wine for this dish, but I liked the fancy crest on the label."

He chuckled softly. "You have excellent taste. This bottle is from my father's collection. I had been saving it for a special occasion and—"

"I'm so sorry," she interrupted. "I can—"

"I was going to say that this is a very special occasion." He met her eyes and held them. "It isn't every day that a man is reunited with his daughter and has a beautiful woman move in with him.''

He liked her blush.

"Thank you," she said in an almost inaudible voice.

"So," he began, trying to keep his tone bland. He was afraid his compliment had made her self-conscious, and he didn't want her to leave. "You saved your salary and decided to take this year off?''

"Not exactly," she said. "My grandparents died within in a few months of each other. After the house was sold and their creditors were paid, I ended up with a little less than a hundred thousand dollars. I'm living off that for the time being.''

"I'm sorry for your loss.''

"Thank you, but it was a blessing. My grandmother had been in a nursing home for years. She'd suffered for far too long.''

"I know that feeling. My father has been ill for quite some time.''

"Does he live here?''

Barrett shook his head as he tasted the pasta. "Father is in Britain. As the Earl of Harley, he has some responsibilities.''

"What's it like being royalty?''

"Fairly dull, I can assure you. You don't usually get to eat food such as this in Britain. This is exceptional.''

"I love to cook. Grandmother was a great cook and she taught me well when I was growing up. I'm probably one of a very few women of my generation who knows how to correctly darn a sock.''

''Does that come up often? Sock darning?''

''Not yet, but you never know. If I run out of money, I can always darn socks on the side.''

''Interesting emergency plan.'' Barrett took a sip of wine, savoring the taste as it warmed his throat. ''Have you told your investment broker that you wish to give up teaching?''

She laughed. ''Look, Your Lordship, people like me don't have brokers. We have tellers at the bank where we keep our money in savings accounts.''

''Safe, but it doesn't really allow the money to work for you.''

''Barrett?''

He was so stunned to hear his name fall from her lips that he nearly dropped his wineglass. He wanted to ask her to say it again and again but he knew such idiocy would probably send her packing. ''Yes?''

''Can we discuss something other than my tenuous financial situation? Why don't you tell me how you become a lord?''

''It's quite difficult, actually. You have to be born.''

''That's it?''

''Well, you have to be born into a royal line. Or, in some cases, the Crown bestows a title on a person later in life.''

''Which are you?''

"I'm royal blood, though it has thinned somewhat over the centuries."

"Does that mean Rachel is royalty?"

"Indeed. In fact, Rachel is actually more important than I, in many respects."

"I don't understand."

"The title Earl of Harley will be passed to me upon my father's death. The family estate passes to my firstborn heir in accordance with a host of traditions and stipulations from my mother's side of the family."

"I thought all British property passed through the firstborn son."

"Most does," he admitted. "But there are exceptions. My father had a title, and my mother's family had the money. This is quite common among royals. They intermarry in many instances to keep lands and titles in various families."

"It sounds confusing."

"You'll get used to it after a while."

"If you're so important, why do you live here instead of England?"

He shrugged. "I went to Harvard to do my MBA. I preferred the business opportunities on this side of the Atlantic."

"Is Rachel a British citizen or an American?"

"Both," he assured her.

Barrett spent the better part of the next hour telling Zoey about his title, his estate in England and his brother, Herbert, and sister, Guinevere—Jenny for short. "Herbert is quite social, but Jenny tends to keep to herself. As soon as she was able, Jenny rented a flat in London."

"I guess all that formality can get to you. I mean, Princess Di hung out with a couple of roommates when she was dating Charles."

"Precisely."

When she got up and placed his plate in the dishwasher, Barrett tried in vain to think of another topic that might keep Zoey from excusing herself for the evening. He had so thoroughly enjoyed talking to her that he would have explained the inner workings of any one of his companies if it meant she would continue to give him her undivided attention.

When she hid a yawn behind her hand, he knew it would be selfish to continue. "I guess we'd better lock up for the night," he suggested. "Come and I'll show you how the alarm works."

"Why?"

"Just in case you have to run out while it's engaged. You don't want to set off the thing for no reason. It *is* quite loud."

Barrett gave her the code and showed her how to override the system, just in case. Then he accompanied her to her bedroom door, much like a man walking a woman home from a date, complete with that awkward moment at the door, that period of indecision when neither party seems to know what to say or do. The walk back to his room felt strangely lonely.

Barrett stripped down to his boxers and sprawled on his own bed. Thanks to Rosita, the room held no reminders of Alice, none but the ones in Barrett's own mind. He had fully expected his first night in this bed to be filled with thoughts of Alice. To his surprise, his mind seemed preoccupied with Zoey. She was so unique, so real...so temporary. That last thought chased him into sleep.

BELLS AND CRIES dominated Zoey's dreams, both growing louder until she finally realized that she was no longer dreaming. She came fully awake at about the same time she heard the commotion in the hallway. Zoey threw back the covers, jumped down off the high bed and raced for the door. As soon as she pulled it open, she blinked in an attempt to adjust to the bright light.

Ignoring the persistent wail of the alarm, she ran to the nursery and grabbed Rachel, then Alex. Holding the infants tightly against her, trying to shield their ears with her hands, she rocked them slowly. Terror edged along her spine when she realized that Barrett was nowhere to be found and that the burglar alarm was still ringing.

Chapter Five

"Barrett?" she called out, frustrated because she knew there was no way she could be heard above the blare of the alarm. Then another thought came to her. What if someone had broken in? She needed to hide. "But where?" she asked. Where could she possibly hide with two screaming infants?

Armed with pacifiers, Zoey miraculously managed to quiet first Rachel, then Alex. That accomplished, she tiptoed down the hallway and into the large closet in her bedroom. With great effort, she balanced the babies in one arm in order to close the door. She could feel perspiration on her face as adrenaline pulsed in her ears. Moving to the side, she ducked between two gowns and twisted so that she was able to slide her back down the cool wall.

Suddenly, there was quiet. The quiet was almost more frightening than the alarm. She could feel the babies relax in her arms, just as she became aware of her own discomfort. Apparently, she was balanced on top of a few pairs of heels, not exactly a comfortable position. The gowns fluttered with each uneven exhalation, and she felt certain that her rapid breathing was at least half as loud as the alarm had been. She waited, wondering at her fate and the fate of the children. Where was Barrett? What was happening?

Over the ragged sound of her own breathing, she heard a series of thuds. Several seconds passed before she realized the thuds were footsteps against the posh carpet. Her heart rate increased. She contemplated calling Barrett's name but didn't dare. If it wasn't him, she shouldn't risk it. She'd give herself away.

She strained to follow the sounds of an approaching person. Then Alex started to cry. Closing her eyes, Zoey patted his back. She felt something hit her thigh and fall to the ground. It had to be the pacifier. She whispered a frustrated curse. Alex's cries grew louder and more insistent. Rachel began to writhe in her arms. It was only a matter of time, she knew, before Rachel would respond in kind.

Zoey was so distracted trying to think of a way to calm the baby that the sudden flood of light caught her by surprise. It also caused a momentary blindness.

"What are you doing?" came the familiar male voice.

"Hiding," she said above Alex's insistent screams. "Help me," she added when she realized there was no way she could stand up with a baby in each arm.

Barrett shoved back the clothing and stood there. His hair was ruffled and Zoey felt her heart flutter when she realized he wasn't wearing a shirt. He loomed above her looking so devastatingly masculine that she finally understood what it meant to get the vapors. She couldn't seem to control herself. She allowed her eyes to feast on the sculpted muscle of his chest, which was covered by rich, dark hair. The hair tapered toward his waist, drawing her eyes to the waistband of his boxer shorts. The sight was so purely sensual that her mouth went dry and an appreciative moan formed in her constricted throat.

"What do you want?" he asked.

Her gaze snapped up to his when the question registered. Had her admiration been so blatant, so transparent? "What?"

"What do you want me to do to help you?"

"Oh," she muttered. "Take Rachel so I can get up."

Barrett did as she asked. His large hands snaked around the wiggling infant. Rachel's squirming body caused the back of Barrett's hand to brush against her. Through the flimsy fabric of her pajamas, she could feel the strength of his hand, feel the heat of his fingers against her breast. The sensation, though brief, was enough to make her gasp.

"What?" he asked. There was an edge to his voice, almost like annoyance.

"I'm sitting on a shoe," she lied.

Rachel was crying by the time Zoey emerged from her hiding place with Alex cradled in her arm. The two babies fell into a kind of rhythm, almost as if their cries were some sort of well-rehearsed chorus.

Zoey led the way to the kitchen, her mind working at full speed. She was keenly aware of his body behind hers. Keenly aware of her attire. Not expecting anything like this to happen, she'd chosen her favorite pair of pajamas. The outfit consisted of a short tank-style top and matching tap pants. The color was a vivid teal and the fabric, what there was of it, clung to her body. It wasn't going to be easy to deal with him when she was dressed like this. She far preferred the empress-style dresses that completely deemphasized her shape. She wore them like a shield against unwanted advances. Not that she believed men would flock to her because of her stunning figure, quite the opposite. She just felt more comfortable, more professional, downplaying her sexuality.

"Why does she do this?" Barrett asked.

"She's probably just annoyed at being awakened by the alarm. What set it off, anyway?"

Barrett didn't meet her eyes when he shrugged. Rachel looked so small in his arms. Seeing the infant nestled against him was both surprising and distracting. Her throat went dry and her mind numbed. It wasn't until that moment that Zoey realized just how big Barrett was. Somehow his seminakedness made him seem even larger, and slightly threatening.

Pushing the unwanted thoughts from her head, she prepared two bottles and handed one to Barrett. Again, their hands touched briefly. Again, she felt that jolt of electricity. It was as if her skin came to life with his touch. That was a very disconcerting realization.

Alex took his bottle greedily, but Barrett wasn't having much success with Rachel. She was still screaming, twisting her head away from the nipple. Barrett's face was wrinkled with concern. Her heart went out to the man.

"Try holding her a little more snugly. Maybe that will help."

Barrett tried several positions, but Rachel's cries only grew worse. Zoey allowed it to continue until she saw tiny tears spill from the baby's eyes.

"I'll change Alex and put him to bed, then I'll give you a hand."

Alex was amazingly cooperative. She burped him, changed him and placed him back in the crib. His little eyes closed almost instantly.

Zoey ran to her room, grabbed her robe and then dashed back to where Rachel was still crying. Barrett looked positively frazzled, and she noted his thick hair was even more rumpled. As if he'd been raking his large hand though it in frustration.

He looked up at her, his expression a silent plea for help. She took the baby and the bottle. The transformation was instantaneous. Rachel's sobs slowed to the occasional hiccup as she took the bottle.

Zoey lowered herself into the closest chair. She smiled down at the now-contented baby. Her smile wavered when she looked up and saw the expression in Barrett's eyes. The frustration was gone, replaced by something completely different. His pupils had grown dark, almost smoldering. His mouth was little more than a thin line. The raw passion she saw there was both thrilling and a little scary. No man had ever looked at her the way Barrett was looking at her at this moment.

The exchange was brief, so brief that when Barrett abruptly turned on his heel and left the room, Zoey wondered if she might have imagined the whole thing.

"Your daddy is a tough one to figure out," she told the baby.

Rachel waved a tiny fist in response.

"Why don't you like him?" she asked. "I have a feeling you might be the first woman in his life to re-act this way, trust me."

It didn't take too long for Zoey to get the second baby back to sleep. Fatigue weighed heavily on her, as did the memory of the strange look she had seen in Barrett's eyes. She decided to get a drink before venturing back to bed. Hopefully, she could catch a few more hours of sleep. The babies tended to be early risers.

The house was now dark, save for a light in the family room. She assumed Barrett must have gone

back to bed. She filled a glass with water and brought
it to her lips.

"Can't sleep?"

She nearly dropped the glass at the sound of his
deep voice. Turning, she found him seated on one of
the bar stools, a small glass partially filled with an
amber-colored liquid cradled in his hands.

"I didn't realize you were still up," she said in a
shaky voice.

"I thought we should talk."

There was a seriousness behind his statement that
caused apprehension to well in the pit of her stomach. "About Rachel?"

He shook his head, took a long sip from his glass
and leveled his gaze on her. His expression was steely,
his jaw set.

"We need to call the police."

It didn't take long for the meaning of his words to
register. "The alarm went off for a reason?"

His nod was slight, which somehow filled her with
a serious dose of trepidation. "Someone tried to remove the screen on the window at the back of the garage," he said.

Her hand went to her mouth. "Oh, my God," she
whispered.

Barrett got up and moved around the counter. His
robe was open so that when he placed an arm around
her shoulders and pulled her to him, Zoey found her
cheek pressed against the soft mat of hair covering his

broad chest. Reflexively, she placed her palm against him, feeling slightly comforted by the feel of well-developed muscle.

"We need to involve the police. There has to be an explanation for all this."

"Alex," she whispered. "Obviously, someone is after Alex."

As he stroked her hair, her nostrils filled with the scent of him. It was a purely masculine scent, a mixture of musky cologne and expensive cognac.

"What do you know about Alex?" he asked.

"I know we can't stay here. I can't put you and Rachel in any danger. I would feel—"

"Hush," he said in a soft command. "I can take care of Rachel and myself. I've already made arrangements for additional security, beginning tomorrow. There's no safer place for the two of you than here in this house."

"But if someone wants Alex, you're putting yourself in a great deal of danger. Why would you do that for strangers?"

"I've got my own reasons," he said gruffly. "Go get dressed and I'll call the police."

BARRETT MADE THE CALL as promised, then pulled on a pair of jeans and a shirt. He was back in the kitchen long before Zoey returned. It gave him time to think about what he was doing. "Keeping her here probably isn't the smartest thing I've ever done," he mumbled into his glass. Still, Zoey had selflessly cared for his daughter; he could hardly turn his back on her now. Barrett frowned. He couldn't help wondering if that was really the reason, or merely the justification. Was it possible he wanted her to stay for a completely different reason? One far less noble?

Responding to a knock at the door, Barrett pressed the appropriate code, disabling the alarm, then opened the door after checking through the peephole.

"Detective Lou Turner," the rotund man in the rumpled suit announced.

The detective and another officer named Fulton came in. Barrett showed them into the family room and offered them seats. Zoey came out a minute later, immediately going to the detective and throwing her arms around his neck.

"I'm so glad you came," she said.

Barrett studied them, trying to determine the relationship. He felt a pang of jealousy until he realized that Zoey had hugged the man in the platonic way of longtime friends. However, his jaw did hurt from clenching his teeth.

She had put on yet another of her shapeless dresses and he had to quell the urge to frown. Now that he had actually seen the outline of her body, he felt even more disdain for her taste in fashion, or lack thereof.

"They called me when they realized there'd be a connection to my open investigation," Lou explained. "Now, tell me what happened."

She looked over at him and Barrett felt an odd sensation. Maybe it was the expectation he read in her upturned face. Or maybe it was just her face, period. Zoey had the ability to send him off kilter. One smile, a small tilt of her head, and he seemed to lose the ability to retain his thoughts. He took a breath and turned his attention to the policeman.

"The alarm went off at about 4:10 a.m. I shut off the alarm, got my gun and went outside." Barrett hadn't expected the small gasp of surprise from Zoey when he'd mentioned the gun. Then he remembered that she hadn't actually seen it. He'd locked it away in the office once he'd assured himself that no one had actually gotten in.

"And?" Lou prompted.

"I walked about the house and that's when I came across the bent screen on the garage window."

"Why did you wait so long to call us?" Lou asked, though his question was clearly directed to Zoey.

"The alarm woke the babies," she explained. "We had to get them taken care of first."

The policeman nodded. "And that bruise on your cheek?"

Barrett noticed Zoey avert her eyes, which resulted in the detective casting a quick, almost damning look in his direction.

"I had a little problem at the store yesterday," she began.

Barrett heard the deceptively positive way she had broached the subject. He didn't know whether to admire her approach or be annoyed that she had talked him out of calling the authorities immediately.

"Describe this problem," the detective asked.

"I think someone tried to take Alex from the grocery cart yesterday."

"What!" the detective bellowed.

"Hush," Zoey admonished. "You'll wake the babies."

"What do you mean you 'think'? Did they or didn't they?"

"She tried, but I had his seat belt fastened, so—"

"Why the hell didn't you call me from the location?"

"It was Lord Montgomery's first day home from the hospital. I didn't want him to have to spend it in a police station, especially since he didn't actually see what happened."

The detective's face and neck had turned an angry shade of red. Barrett shared some of that anger. Perhaps if he'd insisted, they wouldn't be in this position now.

"That's a pretty lame excuse, Zoey," Lou grumbled.

"I would also need to contact Social Services and I was afraid if I told them about the incident, they'd take Alex away from me," she admitted. "Besides, it all worked out for the best. No one was hurt and Alex is safe and sound.''

Even Barrett was having trouble buying her story, and her forced smile.

Lou asked, "If no one got hurt, what do you call that purple spot on your cheek?"

"It's nothing," she insisted, though she nervously twisted several strands of her hair around one finger.

"If you'd have called it in, we might have been able to track down—"

"No one *saw* anything," Zoey interrupted. "Not even me." She went on to give him a sketchy account of what had transpired. The detective's frown deepened as she finished speaking.

"We're running a background on the kid's mother," Lou explained. "The doctors tell me her recovery is progressing at this point. Hopefully, she'll be able to help us sometime soon. Apparently, she's coming out of her coma."

Barrett watched Zoey's expression at hearing such news. It held an odd mixture of relief and sadness and told him that Zoey was very attached to the little boy. Being a foster parent was quite difficult, he decided as he led the policemen to the door.

"My security firm is going to watch the house," he told Lou. For some reason, it was important to convince this man that he was capable of caring for Zoey. Maybe because Lou had repeatedly suggested that

Zoey and Alex would be safer if they moved in with the detective and his family.

"How long have you known him?" Barrett asked when he returned from seeing the officers out and found Zoey fumbling with the coffeepot.

"I've known his wife, Susan, forever. She was my roommate my freshman year. She was a senior, but we got along great. She married Lou right after graduation. I guess that would make it about nine years."

"I see," Barrett replied, amazed by the amount of relief spilling through him. "He seemed pretty irked at us."

She shrugged. "He'll live."

Zoey felt as if she was getting all sorts of different messages from Barrett. One thing was clear, though, and that was his strange insistence that she and Alex stay put. Since the alternative was to be alone with her fears back at the apartment, she wasn't in any real hurry to delve too deeply into his motives.

"If Alex's mother is improving, why don't we try to see her later today?" she asked.

One of Barrett's dark eyebrows arched up in a question. "Investigate on our own?"

"Why not?" she asked. Having voiced her idea, she felt her confidence grow. "Lou said the doctors wouldn't let him talk to her yet, but I'm sure you can get us past the nurses."

He stroked the stubble that had created a dark shadow across his jaw. "What makes you think that?"

he asked as he came around the counter and stood very near to her.

Zoey's pulse reacted to him almost instinctively. She was aware of even the most minute detail. He was wearing a faint half smile and his head was tilted slightly to the side. Even the small bandage which had replaced the gauze pad only added to his aura of strength and power. It wasn't an intimidating power but an attractive one. Her brain finally found the perfect word—the man had magnetism.

"The nurses are rather . . . fond of you," she said.

Barrett slowly moved forward until they were separated by little more than a breath. Zoey lowered her eyes, fearful that her curiosity and anticipation would be reflected there. The scent of his cologne enveloped her. The sound of his breathing was barely loud enough to be heard above the pounding in her ears. She felt a tension grip her, something so palpable that she sucked in a breath and held it, waiting for an unknown release to rid her of this sense of expectation.

He reached for her, closing his hands around her upper arms, pulling her against him. She placed her hands at his waist, knowing full well she should have pushed him away. Instead, she tilted her head back and pressed herself more fully against him.

His breath washed over her face, teasing her slightly parted lips. His eyes were inky, fathomless pools. Slowly, Barrett slid his hands along her sides. When his palms brushed the sides of her breasts, Zoey let out a small gasp. That sound seemed to act as a catalyst. As if in slow motion, he began to dip his head. Lower, lower, until she could feel the heat emanating from his lips. Zoey wanted to pull him down to her, crush his mouth against hers in hopes of quelling the surge of emotion clogging her throat. She longed and she wanted, but it wasn't to be.

As if there was some great master plan to deprive her of such incredible pleasure, the babies began to cry.

Barrett groaned, then rested his forehead against hers. "I guess my daughter hates me more than I thought."

"Barrett?" Zoey said as she stepped away from him. Common sense came flooding back, effectively cooling the passion that had moments before robbed her of all rational thought.

"Yes?"

"Rachel doesn't hate you and this shouldn't have happened."

Having spoken in what she hoped was an even tone, she turned on the ball of her foot and started down the hall. She'd taken only two steps, when she felt his fingers curl around her arm. It wasn't a painful grip, but it was determined enough to stop her in place. Barrett was kind enough not to force her to face him.

"What do you mean?"

"I mean, Rachel just needs some—"

"I'm not talking about the baby."

Zoey felt her shoulders slump. "Okay. This would be foolish of me on so many levels."

"Such as?"

"C'mon, Barrett. How about the fact that we're strangers. Or that we're as different as night and day. Or that you just lost your—"

"I understand."

She felt his hand drop away, but that wasn't nearly as telling as the way his voice had sounded at the merest reference to his wife. Shaken, Zoey raced down the hall as if she was being pursued. In a way, she was being chased, chased by her own guilt.

"Good morning, guys," she said as soon as she entered the nursery. Rachel quieted at the sound of her voice, so Zoey went to Alex first.

She was just finishing up with Rachel's diaper, when Barrett entered the room. His smile was forced but she returned it just the same.

"What can I do to help?" he asked.

"Why don't you take Alex to the kitchen. I'll be right there."

The tension between them was unbelievable. They were stiff and polite, and it was driving Zoey nuts. When they were finally settled, Barrett feeding Alex and Zoey feeding Rachel, she began to speak.

"I think—"

"I'm sorry—"

Zoey smiled. "Go ahead."

Barrett shook his head. "No, ladies first."

"Okay. I think it would be better if Alex and I left."

"And went where? Where would you feel safe, Zoey?"

She shrugged. "I don't know, but I don't think it's fair for you and Rachel to—"

"Rachel can barely tolerate it if I'm in the same room with her."

"She'll get better."

"Until that time, I want you here. I want my daughter to feel settled and secure for once in her short life."

She eyed him carefully. "What about what happened?"

"The attempted break-in or the fact that I attempted to kiss you?"

She felt the blush all the way down to her toes. "The . . . um . . . break-in."

"I'd really rather discuss the kiss."

"Barrett," she groaned. "Please don't make this difficult for me."

"Discussing the fact that I would very much like to kiss you is difficult for you?"

"Yes! I mean no," Zoey stammered as she kept her gaze averted. "It isn't worth discussing."

"Not even a little bit?" he asked.

Slowly, she looked up, finding the smile in his eyes contagious. "Sure, a short discussion is fine. I'll start. It shouldn't have happened, and I would like your word that it won't happen again."

"Okay," he said with a pensive nod of his head. "Short and to the point. It should have happened, I'm sorry we were . . . interrupted and I won't guarantee anything."

"We have to come to—" She stopped when he gave her a silencing look.

"I believe you were the one who said the discussion of our mutual attraction was to be brief. I think we have both stated our respective positions fully."

"Mutual attraction?"

Barrett clicked his tongue. "On to the matter of the attempted break-in. I've thought about your idea of speaking with Alex's mother and I agree it might be of some assistance."

"You do?" she asked. "I mean, good, I'm glad you do."

"I've been thinking," Barrett continued. "Perhaps Alex's father is trying to get him back."

"Maybe, but I'm positive that the person who tried to take Alex out of the cart was a woman."

"Then the father must have someone working with him," he countered. "It's a strong possibility."

"We can go to the hospital as soon as I change."

"What about the babies?" he asked.

"We can bring them along. They don't take up too much space."

He sighed. "We should take extra precautions whenever we're in a public place. The additional security will deter anyone from coming near the house. I don't know about—"

"Have faith," she said as she placed Rachel on the blanket on the floor and took Alex from Barrett. "You might want to move over there, out of the line of fire."

Barrett moved quickly. "Thank you. I don't know how you've managed with these two, given young Alex's propensity."

No sooner had Barrett mentioned it than it became a reality. It amazed her that the child continued to gain weight, since it certainly seemed as if most of his food left him in short order.

After getting things organized, Zoey slipped on her sandals and ran a brush through her hair. She stopped in front of the bathroom mirror, catching the image of herself surrounded by such luxury. Shaking her head, she gazed around the room with a sense of sheer wonder. "I'm starting to feel like Cinderella," she whispered. "And what would I do if Barrett had my glass slipper?" Looking herself in the eye, she answered, "Run like hell."

Zoey carried both babies while Barrett took the newly restocked diaper bag. She followed him through the family room. "Where are we going? Is there some sort of secret passageway?"

"Yes," he called over his shoulder. "It's called the garage door."

"Very funny, Your Lordship."

"Genuflect when you say that."

"Barrett, what's this?" she asked when he flipped on a light and opened the back door of a sleek black Mercedes convertible. She saw that the car seats were safely in place.

"I thought we would all be more comfortable in my car."

"You think I can be comfortable in a car that costs more than my annual salary?" she scoffed. "What if Alex barfs again? I bet it would cost a fortune to—"

"Let me worry about keeping my car clean. Here, give me Rachel, please."

The baby started to whimper in the short amount of time it took him to get her into the car. After snapping the lock on Alex's seat, Zoey reached over and stroked the baby's arm, whispering softly to the little girl.

"Perhaps I should just go ahead and send her to school now," he grumbled as they drove off.

"Send her to school?"

"Of course. I want Rachel to get the same education I received."

Zoey felt her blood begin to simmer. "I take it you went to boarding school?"

"A lovely school in the Lake District. I had—"

"I can't believe you're already planning to send her away. She's not even three months old and you sound like you've already written the tuition check."

"Why are you yelling at me?" he asked.

"Because," she said on an angry breath.

"That's helpful."

"Fine," she said as she turned in the seat in order to glare at his handsome profile. "I can't believe you would send a motherless child off to a boarding school. If she isn't teased unmercifully by her peers, then I can almost guarantee that she'll be homesick."

"Every Montgomery for more than a century has attended boarding school."

"Tradition is dandy, but it isn't nearly as important as making a child feel loved and wanted. You yourself said your own sister is distant. Ever stop to think that all that isolation, as well as having no mother, might have been what kept her from connecting with other people?"

"I think you're turning something completely normal and natural into something that sounds almost diabolical."

"Good word. It *is* diabolical. And cruel and heartless and uncaring and completely against everything we know about children's needs."

"What you Americans know," he countered softly. "There are differences in our cultures. That doesn't make one right and the other wrong. It simply makes them different. Now—" he paused long enough to concentrate on sliding the car into a parking space "—I would appreciate it if you would attempt to remember that Rachel is my daughter, not yours."

Zoey was still hurt and fuming silently when they strolled the babies into the hospital lobby. His words reverberated in her head, a rather unkind reminder that he was absolutely right. Rachel was his and she had no right to comment on his future plans for the child. She was on the verge of telling him just what she thought of his heartlessness anyway, when she looked down at Rachel. The infant's large eyes followed her, as if asking her not to give up on Barrett.

Zoey smiled at the little girl, renewing her resolve to make a caring father out of Barrett before she would leave Rachel. Swallowing her residual anger, she turned her attention to the receptionist.

"What's happening?" she whispered to Barrett.

"Apparently, there's no listing in the computer for Ms. Spears."

"I hate computers," she said, attempting to restore a conversational tone to their exchange.

"I hope others don't share that sentiment. I have a rather large software-development division in one of my companies."

"Oops." Zoey gave him a small smile. "I guess I—"

"May I help you?" a middle-aged man in a suit asked. "I'm Pastor Russell Greavy."

"I don't understand," Zoey said.

The pastor led them down a hall to a narrow room with an altar and pews. He indicated that the adults should take a seat and he stood over them.

"I'm Zoey Kincade and this—" she paused and pointed to Alex "—is Ms. Spears's baby."

The pastor's expression grew solemn. "I wasn't informed that Miss Spears had any relatives," he said.

"Reverend," Barrett began, "is there a problem?"

"I'm afraid Miss Spears succumbed to her injuries this morning. You have my deepest sympathies."

Chapter Six

"Hello?" Barrett said as he balanced the sleeping Alex in one hand, the receiver in the other.

"I've been ringing you forever," the familiar sound of his brother Herbert's voice crackled over the line.

"I've been out," he answered. At the moment, he was being more than slightly distracted by Zoey. She was on the ground, kneeling in front of Rachel. It pulled at his heart to see the way his daughter reacted to the woman. The baby was smiling, close to genuine laughter as Zoey teased her by tickling the child's bare stomach with a lock of long, silky blond hair.

Zoey was not only beautiful, she was competent with the babies. While Alex seemed to accept him, Rachel was still unwilling to allow him to do more than look in her direction.

"Are you sure you're up to flitting about?" Herbert asked.

"I'm fine," Barrett answered. "A tad fatigued, but quite fit, I can assure you."

Zoey turned her face toward him. Her smile was so warm, so genuine that it felt nearly as intimate as a caress. God, he thought, she was certainly something special.

"...have you?"

"Sorry, Herbert, what was that?" Barrett asked.

"You haven't heard from Jenny, have you?"

"No. Is there a problem?"

The pause that followed his question raised some alarm in Barrett. Herbert was normally direct. Anything he had to say was usually delivered promptly.

"Not really. When we got the news about Father, she decided to dash off to London."

"What news about Father?"

He heard Herbert clear his throat. "He's taken a bit of a turn for the worse, I'm afraid. He's back in hospital and the doctors say this may very well be the end."

Barrett sank back against the wall and expelled a breath. The news wasn't unexpected, but it did feel as if a heavy shroud had been placed over his shoulders. "I see."

Zoey must have sensed something by his tone, for she now looked up at him with concern in her eyes. Acknowledging her unspoken communication with a nod of his head, Barrett continued, "Shall I make arrangements to return?"

"Not yet," Herbert answered quickly. "I'll keep you abreast of the situation. Don't do anything until we see how things go."

"But if he's—"

"Rhett," Herbert interrupted. "I don't think it would be wise for you to travel halfway 'round the world. Not when you've just come through a rather trying ordeal."

"But if he has taken a bad turn . . ."

"He's not conscious," Herbert stated. "There's really nothing we can do but wait. Besides, I'm sure it would be a chore to bring the baby over here. You're probably still getting settled with her."

"I have help."

"Ah, you've found a nanny. Good, that should make—"

"Not a nanny," he said, meeting Zoey's gaze. "A friend."

He watched as her tongue flicked out and nervously moistened her lower lip upon hearing his statement. He was rather surprised himself. He'd referred to her as a friend, but what he was beginning to feel was hardly reminiscent of friendship. No, if he had to put a label on it, it would lean more toward desire.

"Is there a problem?" she asked after waiting for him to finish his conversation.

"My father isn't well."

"Oh, Barrett," she said in a soft voice. She was on her feet quickly, moving to his side.

She reached out a tentative hand and wrapped her fingers around his solid upper arm. His height forced her to tilt her head back in order to make eye contact. His dark eyes were sad and reminded her very much of the expression she'd seen that first day at the hospital. He offered a weak smile.

"Is there something I can do?" she asked. "Stay here with Rachel so that you can go see him?"

He shook his head. The action caused a lock of his hair to fall forward on his forehead.

"My brother doesn't feel my presence is required just yet."

She wrinkled her brow. "Not to criticize your brother, but if you feel like going, I think you should go."

Barrett sighed deeply. "The truth is, I don't. I was relieved when Herbert suggested I wait a bit longer."

She gave his arm a gentle squeeze. "If that's how you feel."

His gaze moved away from her eyes, off to a place far in the distance. He looked so sad that it took all her strength to resist the strong urge to circle him with her arms. Instead, she took Alex from him.

"I hate to admit it, but I am troubled by the idea of seeing my father in his current condition. I prefer to remember him as the man he was. I imagine it is difficult for any child to watch the steady decline of a parent."

"It is," she assured him. "What's your father suffering from?"

"Alzheimer's."

Zoey closed her eyes. The memory of her beloved grandmother's futile battle with the unyielding disease was still fresh in her memory. "I'm sorry, Barrett," she said quietly before walking away. This was one topic she didn't feel she could discuss with him, or with anyone. "I'm going to put these guys down for a nap."

A few minutes later, she heard him walk into his office and close the door. Zoey went into the kitchen and decided to occupy herself by making a list of things she needed for the babies. Rachel had outgrown her undershirts and nightgowns. Alex, in spite of the vomiting, had outgrown just about everything. As soon as they woke up, she could drive down to her favorite baby shop. It was one of those huge, warehouse places that sold quality clothing at reduced prices.

She was just finishing her list when the phone rang. She debated answering it, but decided it would be inappropriate. It might be Barrett's brother calling back with even worse news.

After the list was complete, she filled bottles with formula and ran the washing machine. She felt antsy. A few days ago she would have given her eyeteeth for a few hours to herself. Now that she was presented with it, she decided it wasn't all it was cracked up to be.

At her apartment, there was always something to clean. Here, she couldn't even find something to dust. She went into the living room, curious about the art-work and antiques. These things were as foreign to her world as the Mercedes was. Her first thought was that she had no taste in art. She based this conclusion on the fact that she didn't much care for any of the twenty or so paintings hanging in heavy, intricately carved frames. One was so dark and cracked, she couldn't even make out the images. She smiled, thinking it looked very much like the television screen when the cable went out.

As she stepped around a small sofa with ugly striped upholstery, her gaze settled on a small, framed pho-tograph. "So this is the wife," she whispered as she lifted the frame and stared back at the smiling woman.

Alice Montgomery had been a beautiful woman, by anyone's standards. Zoey had expected as much. What she hadn't expected was her reaction to the photograph. She hated the woman on sight. She couldn't help it. She knew from the Social Services file that Alice had attempted to kill not only her hus-band, but also Rachel. Zoey wondered if there might be more behind her strong reaction. Her mind was running a series of images, trying to envision Barrett with his arms around this woman, kissing her, sharing childbirth with her. The mere thought of him with Alice heightened her disdain.

"Can I help you?"

Zoey spun around, guilty and red-faced.

Barrett's expression was stern. His eyes were accusatory, his jaw taut and unyielding.

"I—I was just looking around," she stammered.

"And you just happened to come across a photograph of my wife?" There was a definite indictment behind his words.

"Yes," she answered honestly.

"Rosita was specifically instructed to remove all such items," he said stiffly. "You must really have had to search to find that."

Zoey felt her spine stiffen at his tone. "It was right there," she said, pointing to the place on the end table. "I didn't have to search."

He regarded her for several seconds and she could see the indecision play across his tense features. Shoving his hands into his pants pockets, he glanced away and expelled a breath. "All right."

"Excuse me?" Zoey snapped. "What is that supposed to mean?"

"It means that I accept your explanation."

"Don't do me any favors." Tossing the picture onto the sofa, she stormed from the room. She didn't get very far.

Barrett's hand snaked out and grasped her arm. She refused to react. She was fast learning that this was one of his favorite means of communication. Instead of yanking against his hold, an effort she knew would be fruitless, she stood perfectly still, staring straight ahead.

"Zoey?"

"What?"

"Look at me."

"No, thanks all the same."

"I don't understand why you're so angry."

She made a noise of utter disbelief. Spinning, she looked up at him with angry eyes. "How can you be so dense?"

"Dense?" He repeated the word as if it were new to him.

"You all but accused me of rummaging through your belongings. Then you act as if I owed you an apology."

His eyebrows drew together as if in deep contemplation. "I see where you might have interpreted things in that light."

"Do you have any idea how you sound?" she asked. "You're so stiff, so calm. It's like you're incapable of real emotion."

"That's how I was brought up," he said in a voice that no longer held that edge.

In fact, it sounded as if there was a hint of sadness behind the statement. Upon hearing the unexpected emotion, Zoey felt her anger fade. Turning, they stood toe-to-toe, looking into each other's eyes. She could sense the change, almost feel the new direction their encounter would take. She was suddenly aware that he no longer gripped her arm, but held it. His square-tipped fingers gently brushed the sensitive underside of her arm. With his thumb, he began making slow circles on her flesh. The act was at once innocent and exciting.

Barrett, for all his inadequacy when it came to expressing his feelings, seemed to have no such trouble extracting a physical response from Zoey.

His eyes were so intense, so focused. A small thrill danced the length of her spine when his gaze dropped to her lips. Several charged seconds passed and his attention didn't waver. Her throat went dry when she saw his eyes darken. She stood, fully mesmerized as he lifted one hand. His palm rested in the hollow of her cheek. Involuntarily, her lips parted. Barrett ran his thumb over her lower lip.

She should have stopped it right then and there. She would, she told herself, but she wanted just a few more seconds of the delicious feeling. Just a few more seconds of experiencing his breath washing over her face.

His slightly callused thumb continued the slow exploration of her lip. His eyes remained riveted on his action. His thumb worked its magic, producing a sensation more ardent than any kiss. Her breath stilled in her throat. Her pulse, quick and uneven, raced through her veins, carrying the heat of his touch to every cell in her being.

"Barrett." She whispered his name, still unsure what would follow. Should she listen to her body and ask him for the kiss she so desperately needed? Or should she remind him that this was nothing but a pointless, dangerous game?

Her questions became moot when Barrett dropped his hands to his sides. She found herself looking up into the face of a completely different person. His eyes had narrowed and lost their passion. She was standing there, little more than a quivering pile of hormones, and he appeared totally calm, totally unmoved by what had happened between them.

"Yes?" he asked in an even voice.

She continued to look at him, searching vainly for a lingering sign that he was the same man who had put her through such sweet torture. All traces were gone.

"Nothing," she mumbled as she lowered her head and again started from the room.

"Do we have plans for the afternoon?"

Yes, she thought. I'm going to take an hour-long cold shower to slow my racing heart. "I've got some shopping to do."

"As soon as we—"

"You don't need to go with me. I can handle it."

"I've no doubt you can, but I think it would be safer if we stayed together."

Zoey nodded. "You're right. I think being in this house allows me to pretend that nothing is wrong.

Maybe it would be best if we stayed here. Maybe we shouldn't risk taking the babies out in public."

"I could go for you," he suggested.

Zoey gave a little laugh. "Do you have any idea what Onesies are?"

"I don't have the first notion."

"I could go and you could stay with the babies," Zoey suggested. "I really am to the emergency stage, especially with Alex. He's down to one thing that fits. Today, he's got on one of Rachel's outfits."

"We'll go together, all four of us. How about if I ask the security team to follow us?" Barrett suggested. "I know I'll feel better if there's someone with us, just in case."

Zoey nodded. "I'll get Rachel and Alex ready to go while you take care of the other stuff."

"Zoey?"

She held her breath, hoping he might be about to explain what had happened between them only moments ago. Hoping he could tell her the reason she still felt in the pit of her stomach the lingering effects of his touch.

"Were you expecting any calls?"

"No. Why?"

He shrugged and said, "Just asking."

He offered nothing else, so she went off to get the babies ready for a quick trip to the store.

BARRETT LEFT the two men after explaining his needs fully, and walked back up to the house. His pace was brisk, almost as if he couldn't tolerate these few seconds away from Zoey. He couldn't help making the comparisons. Had he ever felt this way with Alice? Had he ever felt the nearly overwhelming need he felt now? His hand was on the knob as the answer came to him in one quick and succinct syllable—no. Acknowledging that reality, Barrett knew he was presented with the new challenge of finding a way to explore his desires without scaring her off.

He was still distracted by those thoughts as he led the two-car caravan to the place Zoey had insisted they shop.

"...sire?"

"I'm sorry," he said. "What did you ask? And please stop calling me that."

"Sorry," she said brightly, tossing her silken hair over her shoulder. "I asked how you picked the name Rachel."

"That was my wife's...late wife's idea."

He felt her hand at his wrist. Annoyance matured into hostility when he caught a quick look at the expression on her face. She pitied him.

"I didn't realize," she said softly.

Barrett took two deep breaths, trying to keep his emotions in their proper place. "I would appreciate it if you wouldn't do that."

"I'm sorry, Barrett. I really had no way of—"

"Not the remark, that look you wear anytime Alice's name enters our conversation."

He heard her take in a breath. Then, after a pensive moment, she said, "How am I supposed to handle the issue? I don't know what your feelings are."

"My feelings are irrelevant," he told her. "My feelings are my concern."

"Fine."

There was an unfamiliar catch in her voice. Then she stopped looking in his direction. Her face was almost against the window, and he could see a certain stiffness in her posture. It was amazing that he could so enjoy the sexual tension they shared, yet this kind, this emotional clashing, was quite another matter.

"So," he said when he could no longer stand the silence, "what exactly is a Onesie?"

"It's a T-shirt-diaper-cover combo. They're great for the hot weather."

She still wasn't looking at him.

"And why are we going to this particular store?"

"Babies-N-Things is an inexpensive place. I can get more for my money."

She *still* wasn't looking at him.

"Zoey, I no longer expect you to make purchases for Rachel. In fact, I would appreciate it if you would present me with a list of your expenses so that I might reimburse you."

"The state paid Rachel's expenses."

Barrett's frustration increased with the monotone in which she delivered each answer. The woman was positively infuriating. He took a calming breath. "Shall I reimburse the state?" he teased.

"Do what you want."

"Are you always this snippy?" he asked when he could no longer stand her cold-shoulder treatment.

"I'm not snippy. I just don't feel like making small talk with you."

Barrett considered her answer. "Then let's discuss your financial picture." He felt somewhat better when she turned in her seat. Even if she was gaping at him.

"I don't have a financial picture."

"But you could," he said, mildly encouraged that he might have chosen a neutral topic. "I've spoken with my broker and arranged for you to meet with him on—"

"Whoa," she interrupted, raising her hand. "I don't understand what you're talking about."

"I took the liberty—"

"You're very good at taking liberties."

Barrett tried his best to don an innocent expression. "As I was saying, my broker would be happy to see you next week."

"Don't those people charge fees?" she asked.

"Not in this instance."

"That's all well and good, but I can't afford to invest my money. I have to live off what I have."

"He understands that."

"I don't know."

Hearing the indecision in her voice, he added, "I can't think of any other way for you to continue in foster care. I believe my broker can make it possible for you to extend your absence from teaching."

"Okay," she said. "If you think there's a possibility I can do what I want."

"Why do you want to do this?" he asked.

"Because of the kids I met when I was teaching."

"Pardon me?"

"I saw a lot of children who were already in trouble by the second grade. I decided I might be able to do more good if I could reach children before they set foot in a classroom."

"You scoff at the concept of boarding school, but I can assure you, we don't have half the difficulties with our schools as you Americans do."

"Or half the emotion," he heard her mutter.

"How can you say that?" he asked.

"Because of the way you're still avoiding Rachel."

"She's not particularly thrilled with me, either," he reminded her.

"But you're the adult."

"It's just taking me a while to grow accustomed to the role of father."

"You should have thought about that before you had a child."

"It wasn't my decision," he informed her, feeling a tad irritated by her attitude. "I believe we're here."

"Which baby do you want?" she asked.

"Alex." It gave him a small measure of satisfaction when he saw the slight annoyance in her eyes. He knew his daughter wouldn't feel slighted. The baby had still shown no signs of finding him the least bit tolerable.

"I won't be that long," she told him as they carried the babies toward the massive building.

"It looks like a factory," he said. "I thought stores were supposed to have window decorations and such."

"No fancy stuff, just good prices."

Barrett shrugged. The action caused little Alex to burrow against his chest. He felt himself smile as he wondered what it would be like to have a son of his own. A son was expected in his world.

"Why are you smiling?"

"I was just enjoying Alex," he told her.

Zoey's reaction to his statement was quite unsettling. Grabbing his sleeve, she stopped him right there in the center of the parking lot, a short distance past where the security men waited in the parked car. After garnering his full attention, she gave him a brilliant smile. The innocent gesture, over almost instantly, left him smoldering. Had they not been in a public place, he wouldn't have allowed her to happily saunter off. No, he'd have Zoey in his arms, kissing her senseless.

"Coming?" she called.

Shaking off his astonishment, Barrett followed her into the store. It was filled with clothing, shoppers and screaming children of varying ages. He battled the urge to cringe at the unpleasant sounds of mothers berating their children and children throwing nasty little tantrums. Was this what his life was to become? he wondered.

"These are like the ones at the grocery store," Zoey explained as she pointed to a cart. "Put Alex in that seat and fasten the safety cord."

"He can't move," Barrett complained. "What's the point?"

"The point is safety. Now, try to keep up."

Barrett scoffed at the mere notion that he couldn't keep up. How difficult could it possibly be to push a cart through a few aisles of clothing?

"Zoey!" he called as she disappeared down a row well in front of him. Two carts, filled with a variety of clothing and other items, blocked his way. He looked to the woman who had so rudely parked her cart in the center of the aisle and said, "Do you mind?"

"Chill, pal," the woman retorted without even raising her head.

Barrett repeated his question, which earned him a cold stare, though she finally relented. He came upon the second cart and looked around for the elderly woman he had seen an instant before. Great, he thought as he moved his cart gently to the side and walked toward the obstacle, grumbling all the way.

Still not seeing the elderly woman, he pushed the cart far enough into the aisle to enable him to pass.

Turning, he loudly yelled, "Hey!" at the old woman reaching for Alex.

She looked up and their eyes met for a fraction of a second. Then, the white-haired lady ran toward the entrance. By the time Barrett had recovered his wits enough to yell for the manager, the woman was already out the door.

"Yes, sir?" an annoyed woman said as she appeared from the glass-enclosed tower at the front of the store.

"Someone just tried to take this child," he said.

The woman's expression changed as the gravity of his statement obviously registered.

Pulling a clip from her belt, she spoke into a small microphone. "Come with me, sir. We've notified the police."

"I have to find Zoey," he told her. "I have to make sure the other baby is all right."

"Other baby?" she repeated.

"Yes, with Zoey Kincade. She's over there someplace." Barrett pointed in the general direction of where he'd last seen her.

The woman grabbed her handset and mumbled something else. Almost immediately, he heard Zoey's name over the loudspeaker.

"Follow me, sir," the woman said.

Barrett had started after the woman, when he heard yet another woman's voice yell, "Sir!"

His face warmed when he realized that, although he had followed the woman, as requested, he had left Alex and the cart behind. With a guilty smile, he returned for the baby at the same time Zoey appeared, her eyes wide and her lower lip trapped nervously between her teeth.

"What's wrong?" she demanded.

"Someone tried to take Alex," he said. "I'm supposed to go with her."

"God, Barrett. What's happening?"

"I don't know," he told her honestly.

SHE SAT next to him in the small office, cradling Rachel in her arms. Barrett had Alex up on his shoulder. She could see the tension around his eyes and mouth. "It's okay," she said in an attempt to make him feel better. She didn't get any reaction other than a slight grinding movement near his jaw. "This gives us something in common."

"What?"

"Now we've both had the experience of an attem—"

She went silent when she heard the commotion beyond the closed door. The voice was muffled but recognizable nonetheless. Lou Turner burst through the door wearing the same gray suit and the same concerned expression as he'd worn at their last meeting.

"What the hell are you doing in a public place when you know some crazy is after that kid?" Lou demanded.

"We brought security," Zoey told him.

"And left them in the parking lot," he countered as he grabbed a chair, turned it around and threw his booted foot over the top. The chair squeaked in protest when Lou's full weight settled.

"That was my doing," Barrett said. "I thought that since the last attempt had occurred outside the store..." His voice trailed off.

Lou grunted and pulled a small notepad out of his jacket pocket. "Did you get a better look at her?" he asked Barrett.

"She was ten feet away from me," he said. "She was a small, older woman, under five-five, with white hair and—"

"That isn't right," Zoey cut in. "She was tall, with long, dark hair tucked up in her hat. And she didn't seem all that old to me."

"I thought you didn't see the woman that well," Lou said to her.

"I didn't," she admitted. "But I certainly got a sense of what she was like."

"Well, I saw this one," Barrett repeated. "She looked right at me."

Zoey noticed that his eyebrows drew together as if he was struggling with something. "What is it?" she asked.

He lifted his shoulders and said, "I don't know. There was something almost familiar about the woman."

"You've seen her before?" Lou asked hopefully. "This could get us somewhere."

"I think I know her," Barrett corrected. "There was something familiar about her eyes. She looked at me as if she hated me. It was quite unexpected."

"Unexpected?" Zoey repeated, marveling that she was beginning to recognize what she had always heard called British understatement. Only now, she knew firsthand how accurate that description was.

"Can you think of anything?" Lou asked. "Maybe someone from the hospital?" he suggested. "Maybe she was one of your nurses."

Barrett shook his head. "She looked nothing like any of the nurses I came in contact with."

"How about you, Zoey? Did you see anything, maybe someone following you before the two of you got separated in the store?"

"Sorry."

Lou scratched his head and frowned. "I'm getting concerned here. I think you might want to consider taking the baby back to Social Services. He's not your responsibility, Zoey. Let them find a safe place for him."

"What about Barrett's house?" Zoey asked. The whole idea of returning Alex to Social Services was out of the question. "What if I promise not to take the babies out again without security right along with me?''

"I suppose that would work, if Lord Montgomery, here, is game.''

"Of course,'' Barrett said without hesitation. "No problem.''

She caught his eye and offered him a grateful smile.

"You two stay put while I take a few statements from the other shoppers.'' Lou got up and went for the door. With his hand on the knob, he looked directly at Zoey and said, "Please think about what you're doing.'' Then the detective opened the door and left the room.

"He obviously cares a great deal for you,'' Barrett said.

"We're friends,'' she said. "Lou just doesn't understand why I don't take the easy road out on this thing.''

"He believes you should return little Alex to the state.''

She touched his arm and met his eyes. "What do you think?''

"I think Lou's probably right,'' he answered. Then, his eyes softened and he added, "but he's not you. He doesn't share your sense of responsibility to this little boy.''

"Thanks,'' she said as she gave his arm a squeeze.

Barrett stroked his chin. "I hope all of this will be over in short order and it won't be an issue.''

"Good thinking. I wonder how we could have such different ideas of what the woman looked like," Zoey remarked. "Did she have on textured hose?"

"I wasn't looking at her legs," Barrett said. "For a change."

Zoey smiled. "Like mature women, huh?"

"I put that woman somewhere in her late sixties ... though ..."

"What?"

"She ran like a pro."

"Huh?"

"When I caught her near Alex, she turned and ran for the door. She appeared quite light on her feet for a woman wearing those rubbery orthopedic shoes."

"Well." Zoey rose, shifting the now-sleeping baby in her arms. "Maybe the woman was wearing a disguise today. That would explain why she looked one way when I saw her and completely different today."

"What about the height discrepancy?"

"I suppose I could have exaggerated how tall she was," Zoey admitted. "I was on the ground looking up. That's the only possible explanation."

"Did Lou say anything about Alex's father?"

She shook her head. "Not to me."

And he didn't say anything an hour later when he allowed them to leave the store. The manager was apparently so afraid of bad publicity that she insisted Zoey and Barrett accept as a gift from the store the merchandise Zoey had selected. Zoey was grateful, but

Barrett interpreted the offer as a way for the store to ward off unwanted litigation. A police car followed them, along with the rather humbled private-security agents.

It was dark by the time they had the babies fed, bathed and put to sleep. Barrett had been quiet during the process, quiet and distant. Zoey was absorbed with her own thoughts.

As she stood at the counter, mixing formula, Barrett stuck his head around the corner and said, "I'm off to the shower. Do you need anything first?"

"Go ahead," she told him. "I'm going to finish up here and make it an early night. I think all the excitement has finally caught up with me."

He turned to go and Zoey called his name.

"Yes?"

"I haven't really thanked you," she said with her eyes fixed on the design of the tile floor. "Alex and I would be really lost if—"

"Forget it," he said brusquely before disappearing down the hallway.

Frowning, Zoey went back to mixing formula and pouring it into the waiting bottles. The man is tough to figure out, she thought. Maybe it had something to do with the British-title thing. Maybe Barrett's desire to help her came from some ancient sense of chivalry.

"I think that's knights, not lords," she mused with a smile.

The telephone rang just as she was drying her hands. Mindful of the fact that Barrett was still in the shower, she grabbed the receiver and held it to her ear.

"Hello?"

"You didn't listen," the raspy voice said.

"Who is this?" Zoey cried. "Who are you?"

"I'm going to punish you. Both of you."

Chapter Seven

"Calm down," Barrett said as he placed a glass of wine in her hands. "Shall I call Lou?"

"No," Zoey answered in a soft tone. "I'll tell him later. He'll just start on me again."

"What exactly did he say?"

"I don't know if it *is* a man. It's too hard to hear to be sure."

Barrett joined her on the sofa, sitting so close that she could feel the heat of his thigh where it brushed her hip. His hair was still wet. Small droplets of water fell from his glistening dark hair onto his bare chest and shoulders. A good deal of her fear faded as she watched one particular droplet slide over his chest, through the mat of hair, as it moved toward the waistband of his jeans.

He smelled faintly of soap as he lifted his arm and draped it gently across her shoulders.

"I've been thinking," she said.

"I don't think I approve," he teased. "You get rather dangerous when you intellectualize things."

"I'm serious," she insisted, lightly tapping his leg for effect. "I think it would be a good idea if I took Alex and left. There are plenty of small towns in the mountains where we could hide."

His fingers gripped her upper arm as he pulled her fully against his damp chest. "I simply won't allow it."

"You're not thinking," she countered, trying not to give in to the temptation of running her hands over his well-muscled body. "I'm putting you and Rachel in danger by staying here."

"If I believed that, I would have packed the two of you off already."

"We can't stay here, not now."

"What's different about now?" he asked.

"I kept telling myself that the crank calls were the work of some teenage jerk. I can't kid myself now."

"We can have the number changed in the morning. That should put a stop to the calls."

"But not to the cause," she argued.

Barrett gave her another tug, pulling her slightly off balance. Her hand now rested atop his thigh. She could feel and hear the uneven beat of his heart against her cheek. His breath toyed with her hair in a kind of soothing non-caress. His hand had fallen lower, resting right against the curve just below her waist.

"Why are you doing this?" she asked earnestly.

"Because I'm quite intrigued with the shape of your body. Your choice of clothing makes it—"

"Not *this*," she told him, jabbing the back of his hand with her fingernail. "Why are you so willing to help Alex and me?"

Barrett didn't answer immediately. She could feel him stiffen slightly, and his breathing became deeper, more purposeful. After taking one last, deep breath, he said, "Because there was a time in my life when I failed to help someone who obviously needed it very badly."

"Your wife?"

She felt him nod.

"Helping me won't change what happened between the two of you," she warned. "I'm not your wife."

"I do realize that, Zoey. I have never confused you with Alice. Not when I see you with Rachel." He slid his thumb beneath her chin, applying just enough pressure to tilt her face toward his. "Not when I touch you," he said with a softer, seductive tone. "And not when I do this."

She swallowed once, twice as she waited for him to fulfill the promise she saw in his eyes. She saw something else, too. His eyes were smoldering with need. Need as real and palpable as her own.

His mouth loomed mere inches from her own. His eyes were shrouded by half-closed lids. His other hand moved to her face, slowly tracing a finger along her jawline. Zoey's anticipation melded with desire beneath the seduction of his touch.

"May I?" he asked in a husky tone.

Unsure of her own voice, she nodded. His gaze flickered between her lips and her eyes, finally settling on her mouth.

The moment his lips brushed hers, Zoey felt as if a lifetime of longing came to the fore. She became aware of everything. His heat, his scent, his taste. He moved very slowly, the tip of his tongue barely skipping along the obstacle of her teeth. Without thought, she opened her mouth further, savoring the intimacy of the moment.

There was that annoying little corner of her brain still insisting that she push him away. But it just wasn't enough to overcome what she so desperately wanted.

"Zoey," he groaned against her mouth as he raised both hands to caress her face.

It was, she knew, one of those rhetorical things. Barrett wanted nothing more than what she wanted so much to give. Her palms flattened against his chest, over the distended nipples buried in the soft hair. She could feel the tiny ripples as his skin reacted to her touch. It was a heady kind of power, like nothing she had ever dreamed, even in her most secret fantasies.

Her hands moved lower and she felt his sharp intake of breath as she began to explore his body. As if trying to memorize a great sculpture, Zoey fanned her fingers in every direction. When her hand curled around his torso, she contacted something foreign, something that stood out against the smoothness. A scar.

It was the perfect catalyst back to reality. Back to where she belonged. "I'm sorry," she muttered, moving her finger to her lower lip as she moved away from his embrace. "I don't know what I'm doing."

"Kissing me?" he suggested in a voice that was still tinged with passion.

"*Stupidly* kissing you," she said as she rose and opted for the safety offered by distance. With her back against the far wall, she silently pleaded with her pulse to return to normal.

Barrett made no move to go to her, but he did watch her with eyes that reminded her of a predator stalking prey. "I'm sorry you feel that way. I found it a most enjoyable experience."

"I didn't mean it wasn't enjoyable," she clarified. "I think it's way too soon for something like this to be happening between us."

Deep furrows appeared between his eyebrows. Zoey realized she'd been holding her breath, waiting anxiously for his reaction.

The staid, totally controlled incline of his head wasn't at all what she had expected. How could a man kiss her with such passion then accept her rejection without emotion?

"I see," he muttered after a pause.

"Barrett?" she asked, looking up at him expectantly.

He fixed his eyes on hers, his face expressionless. "Yes?"

"I'm very frightened and confused."

"I understand that."

"I think you are, too."

The corners of his mouth curved downward. "That simply is not the case."

"Think," she insisted, moving forward and clutching his arm. "I cannot believe that you have processed what happened with your wife. No person can go through what you did and not have tough memories."

"I believe our arrangement included your assistance with my daughter. My past is none of your concern." He gently pulled away from her hold, rose and placed his hands in his pockets. "Do we understand each other?"

"Yes."

She watched as he disappeared down the hall, silently hoping that he might reconsider. It soon became apparent that Barrett wasn't yet ready to lower that wall he so closely guarded.

RACHEL AWAKENED early the next morning, fretful and slightly warm. Alex seemed to pick up on Rachel's agitation, which meant that Zoey had two infants whimpering before the sun came up.

Placing her lips on Rachel's forehead, Zoey felt her concern multiply. "You're hot," she told the baby. "Let's get your daddy and we'll see what he wants to do. Not that I think he'll have the first clue," she added, "but I think it's appropriate to introduce him to the concept of a medical emergency."

It wasn't anything close to an emergency, but Barrett wouldn't know that. Perhaps the mere thought that his daughter was distressed would somehow evoke an appropriate, fatherly reaction.

"Barrett!" she called as she carried both babies into the kitchen. "Barrett!"

Many of the lights were on as she moved through the house. After taking the children into the family room and laying each on a blanket, she called his name one more time before going to heat bottles. There was an envelope resting at an angle against a small stack of bills. Her name was printed neatly on the outside in a bold, masculine script.

Tearing open the envelope with her fingernail, she yanked the linen note card free and began reading aloud. "Dear Zoey. Herbert rang last night with the news of my father's death. I am on my way to England, where I shall be tending to matters for approximately four days. I have left you the telephone number to the estate and some cash, in case you require anything in my absence. Security will remain at your disposal. Mr. Winters has been instructed to do as you wish while I am away. I will contact you soon. Barrett.''

Zoey expelled a breath and ran her fingers through her hair. So many things raced through her head, she was unsure as to her next move. The babies were crying for food and attention, which forced her back to the present.

Rachel refused to eat and grew more uncomfortable by the hour. Zoey called the pediatrician and her friend Susan while she pulled on some clothes.

''I need to take Rachel to the doctor,'' she explained.

''Is it serious?'' Susan asked.

''I doubt it, but I don't want to take any risks. Is Lou around? I'm afraid to leave the house by myself.''

''Where's the great lord?''

''He had to go to England.''

''He's flitting off for a little R & R and he left you there?'' Susan's words dripped with annoyance and disbelief.

''His father passed away.''

''Oh. Sorry. In that case, Lou and I will be there shortly. Call the doctor's office again and see if you can switch Rachel's appointment to ten. Okay?''

''Thanks,'' Zoey breathed into the receiver.

Susan and Lou arrived as promised and they left for the doctor's office, breaking a very serious rule. Alex was in a car seat, but Barrett had taken his car to the airport, with the baby seats and the stroller inside. Zoey tried to comfort Rachel, who seemed to be in slightly better spirits than when she had begun the day.

"I got another call last night," Zoey said from her place in the back seat.

"Christ, Zoey," Lou bellowed. "How the hell do you expect us to find this broad if you don't cooperate?"

"I am cooperating," she defended. "I'm telling you all about it."

"Was it the same voice as before?" Susan asked.

"I think so."

"This doesn't make any sense," Lou said. "If she's trying to grab the baby, why the threatening calls?"

"I don't know. But this time, Barrett was included."

"WOULD YOU CARE for tea, sir?" Maxwell asked as he stood crisply before him, balancing an ornate silver service.

"No thank you," Barrett answered.

Herbert answered, "Yes."

After the butler had poured the tea and left the room, Barrett regarded his younger brother as they sat in matching wing chairs in the drawing room of his family's ancestral home. "Any luck reaching Jenny?" he asked.

Herbert nodded. "She took the news rather hard, you know. She said she couldn't even handle coming out for the funeral. She'll call you later in the week, as soon as she pulls herself together.''

Barrett nodded and gave a nervous tug to the lapels of his dark suit. ''I hope she'll change her mind before the service. I think later on in life she might regret not having accepted the opportunity to say a proper farewell to Father.''

''I've taken the liberty of beginning the process for the funeral.''

Barrett gave his brother a sad smile. ''Thanks.''

''Is someone bringing Rachel over?'' he asked.

Barrett shook his head. ''No. I thought it best that she remain behind.''

''I've missed seeing her,'' Herbert said. ''I'm sure she's grown considerably since...''

''You can say Alice's name,'' Barrett assured his brother. ''She seems very much like a part of my very distant past now.''

''How is that?''

Barrett shrugged and wished he'd had a brandy for fortification. ''I have met someone.''

''Rhett?'' Herbert cautioned. ''Aren't you being a tad rash?''

''Probably,'' he admitted. ''Zoey is a very unusual woman.''

''Zoey...?''

''Kincade,'' he supplied. ''She's the woman who cared for Rachel while I was recovering.''

"I still don't see why you wouldn't allow me to bring Rachel here while you were in hospital."

Barrett was sad to see that his brother still harbored ill feelings over that decision. "She was only a few weeks old," he reminded Herbert. "I was strongly advised against such a long trip for such a small baby."

"Yes, yes," Herbert said as if he didn't care to rehash the issue. "And you find yourself with feelings for this Kincade woman?"

Barrett shrugged. "I think so. But there are many complications."

"Such as?"

"She's a foster parent. Very committed."

Herbert nodded. "Have you told her yet that you don't care for children? Is she aware that Rachel was only conceived as yet another way for Alice to torture you?"

"WHAT DID the doctor say?" Susan asked as soon as Zoey had carried the baby out of the examining area.

"He can't find anything wrong. Her ears, everything is clear."

"Good. I'm taking you and the babies back to my place until we can figure out where to go from here."

"Thanks," Zoey responded as she hugged her friend. "I'm really scared and I don't think I want to go back to the mausoleum just yet."

"Is it that bad?" Susan asked as they entered the parking garage adjacent to the medical center.

The two security officers, who had been leaning against their nondescript black sedan, quickly got in their car. "I feel like some sort of Mafia princess," Zoey admitted. "Those security guys never smile or anything. It's like having two zombies outside."

Lou drove them to the home he shared with Susan. He stayed long enough to give them instructions about staying put, before he went out to speak to the security team.

"What about the lord?" Susan asked. "How are the parenting classes going?"

Zoey gave a humorless little laugh. "I think I'm getting more of an education than he is."

"Hold on," Susan said as she brought two mugs of coffee to the cluttered table. "What are you saying?"

Zoey twisted a lock of her hair around her finger and kept her eyes averted.

"This is serious," Susan groaned. "You never twist your hair unless you're super uncomfortable. What's up, Zoe? What's happening between the two of you?"

"Nothing, really," she hedged. "It's just a little strange being in a house alone with an attractive, sexy man."

"Who just lost his wife," Susan retorted, clearly annoyed.

"Why are you mad?" Zoey asked.

"Because I was afraid something like this would happen. I'm the one who has always believed that men and women can't really be friends. And anyone who says they can, doesn't have a sex drive."

"Susan!"

"It's true—and apparently you and the lord have perfectly functional libidos."

"It isn't like that," Zoey insisted. "It's been more looks than actual contact."

"How serious was this actual contact?" Susan asked.

"A short, little kiss. That's all."

Susan glared at her with a mixture of disapproval and sorrow. "You ought to know better."

"You're acting like I'm having mindless sex with the man."

Susan shook her head. "I'm just not willing to sit by and watch you do something this stupid. Given his last experience, do you think he'll be in any great hurry to get married again?"

"No," Zoey conceded.

"Do you think you'll be able to have an affair? Are you going to be content spending a big hunk of your life caring for an overprivileged baby? Rachel is great, but you told me you were leaving teaching because you wanted to make a real difference."

"Okay," Zoey said when she could no longer stand hearing all the negative possibilities of any relationship with Barrett. "You're right, I'm playing with fire."

"So, what are you going to do?" Susan asked.

"I'll be more professional. I'll make sure there isn't any opportunity for anything to happen between us."

"That's not going to work," Susan warned.

"What do you suggest, then?"

"Move out, distance yourself. If you're attracted to the guy, I don't see how you can live under the same roof and keep your relationship platonic."

"I can," Zoey insisted. "I can't leave now, I have to think of Rachel's well-being."

"You're not the kid's fairy godmother," Susan countered.

Sighing, Zoey let her shoulders fall forward. "She doesn't have anyone else. If I can't get through to Barrett, if I can't make him feel comfortable around the baby, then I know Rachel will be shipped off to some fancy boarding school by the age of five."

"How can you know that?"

"He told me."

"HELLO?"

"I know you're alone," the voice said.

Tears of frustration burned her eyes as she slammed the receiver repeatedly on the cradle before depositing the phone on the table. Her nerves were near the breaking point.

Walking through the darkened house, she went to the foyer and carefully peered through the sheer curtains. The security car was still out front and she could see the two men watching the house. She knew, too, that there was a second team, one that guarded the secluded backyard. She thought about going outside.

Barrett had left in such a hurry that he had never gotten around to changing the telephone number.

Tugging at the corners of her robe, she wondered if she should call him, ask how much longer he expected to be in England. Taking a series of calming breaths, she tried to rid her mind of the repetitious torture of replaying the frightening words spoken by the faceless voice. It was a difficult task. This was the fifth call in as many days. Whoever was on the other end knew exactly what was happening at the Montgomery house.

That wasn't all that difficult, she reminded herself. News of Barrett's father's passing had made all the papers as well as notable mention on all the national news programs. A photograph of Barrett's handsome face had smiled at her numerous times since his departure. Usually, he was identified as the new Earl of Harley as well as the victim of a mentally unbalanced wife.

"I wonder if what Alice did to him will follow Barrett for the rest of his life? Or Rachel," she added as she tossed off her robe and climbed onto the bed. Maybe Susan was right, maybe there wasn't anything she could do that would turn the Montgomerys into a functional family. Especially since she'd learned that Barrett's new title would require him to attend functions in Great Britain from time to time.

Folding her arms behind her head, she stared at the pattern of moonlight and shadowy leaves on the ceiling. With the receiver off the hook, Zoey was able to eventually fall asleep.

The sound that awakened her was totally unexpected. Shaking the last vestiges of sleep from her brain, she sat up and listened. "A thud," she whispered in the early-morning quiet.

Jumping off the bed, she didn't bother with her robe. Instead, she slipped her slightly trembling hand beneath the mattress and box spring and retrieved the kitchen knife that she had placed there for just such emergencies. Silently, she cursed the fact that she didn't have a telephone extension in her bedroom. She knew she had to get to the kitchen or the front door.

It was still well before dawn when Zoey eased her way out of the bedroom. Staying close to the wall, she inched along, holding her breath. Fear had her pulse exploding in her ears, but she still managed to hear the faint sounds of the thuds coming from the rear of the house. She held the knife ready, her gaze darting ineffectually in the darkness.

With her teeth tightly clenched, she locked and closed the door to the nursery after assuring herself that the babies lay undisturbed. Feeling the perspiration on her skin, she turned and tiptoed toward the door, toward the security guards. She was getting closer, twenty feet, then ten. Adrenaline rushed through her system, causing her to shake. The door was finally in sight and she quickened her pace.

She had touched the knob, when a large hand clamped down on her shoulder.

Chapter Eight

Her scream nearly drowned out Barrett's yelp of pain.

"Good Lord, woman!" He wrapped the curse around the finger that he held to his lips.

"Barrett!" she wailed before flinging herself against him. "You're back."

"Is that why you stabbed me? Some sort of new greeting I'm not familiar with?"

"I'm so sorry," Zoey said, placing a hand to her mouth. "How bad is it?"

"I've had worse paper cuts."

Looking down at the object in her hand, Zoey regarded the knife as if it was the first time she had seen it. Horrified by her own actions, she hurriedly rid herself of the weapon.

"You look tired," he said when she brought him a damp cloth to tend his injured finger.

"I am," she admitted with a small smile. "How bad is it, really?"

"It's fine, see?" Barrett displayed his finger, which showed only a small nick by his knuckle.

Relief washed over her to see that it wasn't bleeding any longer.

"What's with the knife?" he asked.

"It's been a rough week."

Zoey regarded him quietly, taking in the sight of him. It was enough to make her breath catch in her throat. His hair was damp and ruffled. His chest bare and glistening. A towel hung around his neck, falling over his shoulders to his waist. The top button of his jeans had been left undone, inspiring any number of fantasies. With his head tilted to one side, his eyes studying her, Zoey felt her knees buckle.

"I didn't know you were coming back."

"I tried to ring you, but there's something wrong with the telephone."

"Me," she admitted. "I left it off the hook."

"More trouble?"

"Uh-huh." She lowered her head, trying to decide how much she should say.

"Have you contacted the police? Kept them abreast?"

"Yes. I've spoken to Lou every day, sometimes twice."

After a disgusted shake of his head, Barrett reached out and took her hand in his. "Let's have a drink."

"It's four in the morning," she said, but it wasn't really a protest.

Zoey tried not to watch the play of muscle as he walked. She forced her eyes lower, but that had disastrous consequences. His rear end was just as impressive. She swallowed, trying hard to remind herself of her conviction not to give in to the major temptations that seemed to eclipse everything whenever he was around.

Barrett poured them each a drink and motioned Zoey to follow him into the family room. She purposely selected one of the chairs and watched, wide-eyed, as he settled on the sofa, resting his elbows on his knees. The tumbler was gripped firmly between his large hands. His dark eyes held hers.

"How bad has it been?" he asked.

"Pretty bad. I haven't been out of here, except to take Rachel to the doctor, since you left."

"That explains the knife," he said with a wry smile.

"Don't you want to know why I took Rachel to the doctor?"

Barrett blinked, then said, "Of course."

"It must have been a bug, or something."

"Good."

"No." Zoey sighed. "Your next question is supposed to be, is she all right now?"

"Is she?"

She tried to stifle her irritation, keeping her voice steady. "She's healthy as a horse, now."

"Did Alex suffer any ill effects?"

Staring at him, she wondered at the man. He seemed to know the right thing to say when it came to Alex. Why couldn't he apply that tact to his own daughter? "Alex is fine."

"Good," Barrett said with a small smile.

"I saw a lot of you while you were away." Keeping her eyes fixed on him, she took a sip of her wine.

"The press was rather intrusive."

"What are your plans?"

"Plans?" he asked.

"They said you'd have to stay in England now that you're the earl."

"I will have additional responsibilities," Barrett conceded. "But for the time being, I can commute. Thanks in large part to the miracle of the fax machine."

"Do you want to move back to England?" she asked. It would make perfect sense. It wasn't as if he'd had a great life in America.

"Not particularly. Herbert can handle many of my duties. He's more than willing."

"That's nice."

She wanted to keep him talking, wanted to know every detail of every minute of his trip abroad. Like most Americans, her knowledge of British royals was limited to the bits and pieces delivered via the news or the grocery-store tabloids. Sadness came when she thought of Rachel. She hated the idea that the little girl would be raised in the impersonal world of boarding schools and nannies. Children, she knew, could overcome a lot if they received love and attention.

"I'm rather tired from my trip," he said.

Reluctantly, Zoey sighed and rose. "I'd better get some sleep, as well. Those guys are usually awake at first light."

Zoey's prediction was accurate. The cries began as the soft charcoal black of morning gave way to a hazy dawn. Taking Alex out of the crib, she talked to Rachel in a soothing tone while she tended to the little boy.

"Your daddy's back," she called over her shoulder as she ripped the tapes on Alex's diaper.

Rachel's cries seemed to intensify upon hearing the news. Impossible, Zoey thought. There was no way that an infant not yet three months old could understand the meaning of those words. "Sorry I mentioned it," Zoey said.

"Mentioned what?" Barrett asked as he appeared in the doorway.

He looked relaxed and very sexy wearing only his jeans and a half smile.

Lifting Alex onto her shoulder, she moved toward him. "Change Rachel and bring her into the kitchen."

"Wait," he exclaimed.

She peered up to find him looking very nervous at the prospect. "No staples this time," she reminded him.

"But—"

"Hurry up," she said sweetly. "She's hungry."

Zoey cringed as she listened to Rachel's incessant screaming. She had both bottles heated and she was seated, feeding Alex, by the time a very harried, very sweaty Barrett arrived.

Rachel hadn't fared much better. The baby was red-faced angry. Her tiny fists waved in the air, occasionally contacting Barrett's bare chest.

"Her bottle is right there," Zoey called. The set of his jaw told her almost as much as the narrowing of his eyes.

"Please trade with me," he pleaded when he joined her in the family room.

"No way."

"For God's sake, woman, I can't deal with—"

"You need to learn," she cut in. "It won't get any easier if you keep avoiding her."

Rachel wouldn't take the bottle. Barrett chased her mouth with the nipple, but to no avail. Zoey waited, silently hoping that Rachel would relent. It wasn't to be. Expelling a breath, she finally said, "Give her to me."

Barrett couldn't hand the baby over fast enough. He willingly, almost urgently, grabbed Alex and backed away. It was as if he feared Zoey might change her mind. Rachel's reaction was nearly as extreme. Her cries subsided almost immediately.

"I don't know what you were trying to prove by that little stunt," Barrett said.

His voice was hard, angry and dripping with condescension.

"She's your daughter," Zoey replied.

"But you're here to—"

"Help with the transition," Zoey finished. "Not act as your baby-sitter."

His eyes grew more dangerous as he asked, "Is this some sort of retribution because I had to go to my father's funeral?"

"Of course not," she scoffed. "Now that you're back, we have to start working on building a relationship between you and Rachel."

"Not bloody likely," he grumbled just as Alex barfed all down his back.

Zoey did manage to keep from laughing until after Barrett had left the room.

"I'VE MADE arrangements for you to meet with Greg Higgins, my broker, next Wednesday."

"If you think it's worth it," was Zoey's reply. She was tired from a day that was punctuated by a battle of wills between herself and Barrett. He'd resisted almost all of her suggestions regarding Rachel and had actually yelled when she announced he would be responsible for bathing the little girl.

"Did you have something else planned?" he said.

"No. Unless I decide to leave before then."

"Why would you do that?"

She made a disgruntled sound. Regarding him across the span of the counter, she shook her head gently. "Things aren't exactly working out here."

He pondered her answer for a moment, then asked, "Why do you say that?"

"We're not getting through to each other."

"I'm trying," he said defensively.

His chest inflated as he became slightly indignant, making him appear even bigger. There were small lines around his eyes which she suspected were a direct result of his daughter's continued rejection.

"Not in my opinion."

"That's silly," Barrett said.

"No, it's the truth. Just like it's true that you have only done what I've asked. Not once have you ever approached Rachel without my direction. What is your problem? Why are you so comfortable with Alex and so uncomfortable with your own daughter?"

"Alex doesn't hate me."

"Neither does Rachel."

"Then why does she cry whenever I come near her or try to touch her?" he snapped.

"Probably because she senses how you feel about her."

"And exactly how do I feel?" he snapped.

"You don't have a paternal cell in your body," she answered with equal force.

"I never claimed I did." Barrett raked his fingers through his hair. "I think you're hell-bent on making me—"

Barrett was silenced by the ring of the telephone. Zoey thought he might rip it off the wall when he grabbed it with such fury.

"What!" he barked. After a few seconds, he yelled, "Who the hell are you?" Another pause, then, "Blast you!"

Zoey blinked at the barely contained rage she saw in his eyes. Barrett looked positively violent when he slammed the receiver back onto the cradle. His breath came in short spurts as he stood there, opening and closing his fists.

"Our friendly caller?"

"I imagine it's the same person, only this time, they didn't hang up."

Her eyebrows drew together when she absorbed what he had said. "What are you talking about?"

Sighing, Barrett said, "I received one other call."

"When?"

"The first night you were here. I heard some heavy breathing, then the line went dead. I have always assumed that it was your tormentor."

"We should call Lou. He said that he would see about putting a tap on your phone as soon as you were back in town."

Barrett nodded. "Let's give him a ring."

"He's at home," Zoey supplied. "He's off duty."

Lou arrived just shy of an hour later. He greeted Zoey with a hug. He acknowledged Barrett with a combination of respect tempered with caution. Zoey knew immediately that Susan must have told Lou about the kiss.

"Have you made any progress on finding Alex's father?" Barrett asked.

"Not yet, but we've got the name of one of his mother's friends. Hopefully, she can lead us to the father."

"Zoey said you wanted to do something with the telephone?" Barrett said as he handed Lou a bottle of beer.

"We'll put a tap on the line to see if we can find the caller."

"I have another suggestion," Barrett said.

"What?"

Zoey leaned forward in her chair, fully expecting him to say he wanted her and Alex out of his house before morning. Holding her breath, she waited, scared, but knowing it was probably the only sane thing for him to do.

"What if I take Zoey and the babies away from here? Somewhere where we can blend in until you get to the bottom of this."

Lou grunted. "Just where do you think a couple with two infants won't be noticed?"

Barrett smiled broadly and said, "Disney World."

TWO DAYS LATER a cab delivered Barrett and his entourage to the Grand Floridian. He'd selected this hotel for two reasons: the Victorian-themed hotel had abundant security and it was huge. It would be easy for the four of them to blend in here.

"This is incredible."

He had to smile at the way Zoey peered around, her eyes wide with what he could only describe as wonder. Something had happened to her almost the instant the chartered plane left Maryland. It was like seeing a great weight lifted from her shoulders. It also made her seem all the more beautiful to his eyes.

"I'm quite glad you approve."

"That's an understatement," she told him as she took Rachel out of her car seat. "Look at him," she said with almost childlike excitement.

Following the finger she pointed, Barrett saw the greeter by the door. He was dressed in a period costume, welcoming hotel guests with a tip of his hat. "I'll get Alex," Barrett said.

"Wait," she said, touching his arm. "Take her."

"Zoey," Barrett began to argue.

Lifting her chin, she looked at him with such expectation in her eyes that he simply couldn't say no. Glancing around at the steady stream of people, he cautiously slipped his hand beneath the sleeping baby's head.

"Careful," Zoey whispered.

To his utter amazement, Rachel didn't cry. She also didn't wake up, but he was willing to overlook that small detail.

With the slender, credit card–shaped keys in his pants pocket, Barrett ushered the group up to the top floor of the elegant hotel.

"Oh, my heavens," he heard Zoey gush as soon as they stepped inside the suite. "I feel like I'm playing Jo in *Little Women*."

"I believe Jo was younger," he teased, enjoying the playful way she offered her tongue.

With the bellman tipped and gone, Barrett stood in the center of the living area, still holding his sleeping daughter. Zoey exploded into a flurry of activity. He followed her with his gaze as she moved in and out of the three-room suite.

Instead of wearing her normal, decidedly frumpy attire, she had on a pair of tailored shorts in one of those feminine colors that he could never remember. Taupe, mauve, or whatever the fashionable term was for beige. Her shapely, attractive legs drew his eyes. Other than those few occasions when he'd seen her in her pajamas, this was his first real opportunity to openly admire her.

Without the fear and threat of harassing phone calls, Zoey's posture had changed dramatically. Her movements were relaxed and fluid. She reminded him of a trained dancer, long legs and dainty movements. She'd piled her hair on top of her head, leaving only a few strands free at her nape. The sight of her smiling profile caused stirrings of desire to enter his conscious mind.

"You can put her down now," Zoey whispered as soon as she had arranged the crib to her satisfaction.

Barrett put his daughter to bed without waking her. He felt a sense of accomplishment, a feeling bolstered by Zoey's approving smile.

"I feel like I should give you some sort of diploma," she said.

Barrett returned the smile, though he could think of many things he would like from Zoey and a diploma wasn't among them. He followed her from the bedroom, quietly closing the door on the way out.

"This is so cool," she said as she went to the window and peered out.

Barrett went to stand behind her, taking in the unobstructed view of the Magic Kingdom just across the water. "I thought you might enjoy it here."

"I've never been before," she said with genuine excitement in her voice. "It's like a dream come true."

"I'm glad you approve."

She turned then, her face lifted, her eyes large, her smile warm. "I feel so much better."

The scent of lilacs teased him. "I thought we were all in need of a bit of a break."

He wanted to reach out and brush the strand of silken hair from her cheek. Perhaps touch her warm skin, caress the soft angles of her jawline. Standing there, outlined in the golden beauty of the Florida sunshine, Zoey was without a doubt the most fascinating creature he had ever encountered. She was so real, so genuine. So perfect.

"The calls and things were getting to me." Her voice had dropped an octave. It was now smooth and sultry, and caused a tightness in his gut.

"We shouldn't have any troubles down here," he assured her. "Only a handful of trusted people know we're here."

"Were you able to reach your brother and sister?"

"I spoke with Herbert. Apparently, Jenny is still locked away in her London flat."

Their eyes met and Barrett experienced an almost palpable current. He suddenly became aware of everything. She was close enough so that he could feel the heat emanating from her body. He could hear an even rhythm as the gentle slope of her breasts rose and fell with each breath. The temptation to reach out and pull her into his arms was strong.

"Why are you looking at me like that?" she asked.

"I think you know."

Indecision clouded her eyes, but only for an instant. Then, with only a measure of hesitation, her hands found his.

"This isn't a very good idea," she told him.

"Why is that?"

Her fingernails teased the sensitive skin on the back of his hand. It made concentration something of a chore.

"Susan reminded me of the dangers of getting involved with a man like you."

"I hate Susan," he replied.

"She isn't real thrilled with you, either," Zoey told him, though there was no real malice behind her words.

Or maybe there was, but he was having difficulty focusing on anything beyond the feel of her skin.

Turning the tables slightly, he laced his fingers with hers and brought her hands up next to her head. In the same motion, he took a step forward, so that his body pressed fully against hers.

Swallowing a groan, Barrett reveled in the sensations. He could feel the soft fullness of her breasts, the firmness of her bare thighs. It was more than enough to push him over the brink. However, it was the expression in her eyes that was his final undoing. There was no way he could restrain himself when he saw unfulfilled passion swimming in their watery depths.

"I guess there's no way we can avoid this, huh?" she asked.

Her voice was little more than a breath. He felt a surge of desire rip through him, carrying heat to every part of his body.

He released her hands and pulled the pins from her hair. The fastenings clattered to the floor unnoticed as he arranged her hair around her shoulders.

"Do you want to avoid this?" he asked, holding his breath for her answer.

Shyly, she shook her head as her hands went to his waist.

"Good," he murmured.

Taking her face in his palms, Barrett whispered her name. It seemed to echo in the stillness of the grand room. He felt intensely nervous, a feeling he hadn't experienced since the awkward days of his youth. Something about Zoey always managed to keep him off-kilter.

Locking his gaze with hers, he allowed his fingers to trail down her cheek, across her jaw. Her skin was warm, flushed, her lips parted. Her breathing became more uneven and the mere sound of it caused a tightness in his groin.

One finger slid lower still, to the soft skin near her collarbone. He stopped long enough to tease the hollow curve at the base of her throat. He smiled when a small moan slipped past her moistened lips.

Need was an urgency so fierce that he wondered if he would be able to manage an appropriate seduction of this lovely woman. The desire to simply tear away the barrier of her clothing was overpowering.

Barrett sucked in a breath as he battled for control.

His fingers found the tiny button at the top of her blouse. His eyes became fixed as he opened the first button, then the second. Her skin was flawless, flushed. She closed her eyes as his fingers explored the valley between her breasts.

She made a small sound as his palm disappeared into the folds of her shirt. Cupping the fullness in his hand, Barrett wondered again how much of this he could stand before his own control shattered. Touching Zoey was like touching heaven. It was sweet, thrilling and more exciting than anything he had ever experienced.

Inclining his head, he brushed her lips with his own. Tentative at first, then more insistent as his need grew more demanding. The feel of her hands wrapping around his waist, urging him closer, was purely erotic. As was her gasp when he pressed his hardness into the softness of her flat stomach. Wrapping his fingers in her hair, he gently forced her head back even farther as his hand kneaded her swollen breast.

Lifting his head, he said, "You're amazing."

"Thank y—"

A cry cut off her words.

"No," Barrett groaned. "Maybe they'll quiet."

After a small shove, Zoey ripped herself from his hold, leaving him feeling frustrated.

"They haven't eaten for hours," she told him in a raspy voice.

Looking toward the ceiling, Barrett silently prayed for strength. Parenting, he decided, was very inconvenient.

ZOEY WAS SURE she could have used her own body heat to warm the bottles. Her pulse was still ragged as thoughts and images raced through her mind. One thing was crystal clear. She had absolutely no self-control when Barrett was around. Her behavior minutes earlier was so out of character. What is it about him? she wondered. Why do I completely lose it whenever he touches me?

Having warmed the bottles in the small kitchen, Zoey went back into the sitting area, where Barrett was doing his best to manage both babies. Zoey didn't meet his eyes when she asked, "Which one do you want me to take?"

"Rachel," he answered without hesitation.

"But you did so well when—"

"Just take her," Barrett fairly barked.

"Fine." She sighed as she took the little girl. "It isn't her fault," she told him as soon as she had taken a seat and given Rachel the bottle.

Barrett sat across from her, with Alex balanced on his knees hungrily sucking on the bottle. "Did I say it was?"

"You're acting like it."

"That's absurd," he responded crisply.

"Then why are you in such a vile mood?" she demanded.

He leveled his dark, brooding eyes on her and said, "Because I would much prefer being in bed with you than sitting here, preparing to be vomited upon."

Zoey felt a small thrill dance along her spine. "It didn't work out that way."

"It should have," Barrett grumbled.

Zoey waited a few minutes, hoping he might calm down a bit before she spoke again. "Maybe not."

"Maybe not what?"

"I don't think it would be a good idea for us to sleep together."

"Is that why you were moaning when I had my hand down your shirt?"

Zoey felt the heat on her cheeks. "You don't need to be crass."

"Then don't try to tell me you weren't with me one hundred percent."

"I wasn't saying that," she said. "But now that I've had a chance to think about it, I came to the conclusion that it's not such a hot idea."

"I think you're embarrassed because you want me."

"I think you have a massive ego."

"Really?" he asked in a low, challenging tone. "As soon as we've finished with these babies, want to put my theory to the test?"

"No," she answered quickly. "I was trying to tell you that I don't want that kind of involvement with you."

"Did you decide that before or after I touched you?"

"Please stop making this so difficult."

"Tit for tat," he said. "No pun intended."

Zoey struggled to keep her temper. She knew Barrett was baiting her and she refused to go for it. She decided to take a different tack. "I would be a liar if I said I wasn't attracted to you."

"Now we're getting somewhere."

"But," she added quickly, "I don't want anything to happen."

"Given how we react to each other, do you really think that is possible?"

"Yes. We're not animals. We don't have to act on every impulse."

"So, what do you suggest we do?"

"We have to agree not to act on how we feel," Zoey said, hoping her voice sounded stronger than she felt.

"Fine."

Barrett's quick agreement was followed by hours of what she could only call sulking. He avoided her as if she had a communicable disease. If she tried to draw him into conversation, she was treated to a noncommittal grunt or shrug. If she asked for his help, he did exactly what she said, with no conversation and absolutely no eye contact. In short, she thought he was acting like a spoiled jerk.

"I'm going to take the babies out for some air," she said when she couldn't stand one more minute of his look-right-through-you stares.

With Alex and Rachel strapped into the stroller, Zoey left the suite so that Barrett could be alone with his nasty mood. "Your father is a pain," she told Rachel as they walked toward the elevators.

The scent of fresh flowers hung in the air, wafting up from the open lobby below. Zoey pressed the elevator button, then stepped over to the polished brass railing and peered down at the beautiful decor below. People swarmed in and out of the huge area, dressed in everything from theme clothing to fancy sportswear. The screams of excited children melded with the hum of a dozen private conversations and the gentle tinkle of a piano.

Zoey's eyes went from place to place, drinking in the beauty of the hotel. She loved it all, the flower arrangements, the gilded mirrors, the efficient, costumed staff. She took a deep breath, realizing that she felt free for the first time in days and days. Glancing back, she checked the stroller and the progress of the elevator, then returned her attention to the scene below.

She smiled at a small child skipping across the marble floor with several large balloons tied to her wrist. Yet another man carried a huge stuffed doll. The sound of the elevator opening pulled her away from the railing.

After a brief struggle with the wheels of the stroller, Zoey managed to get herself and the babies into the elevator. She hummed along with the show tune playing inside the compartment. She was feeling better with each passing second. His Lordship could stay up there and pout all day and night, for all she cared. She was going to enjoy this opportunity. She would walk the children out by the water, eat something, then maybe sit and watch the fireworks display over at the Magic Kingdom.

The elevator doors slid open, and she started to push the stroller forward. Then her eyes fixed on the sight before her and a scream formed in her throat.

Chapter Nine

"Yes, ma'am?" the employee said as he weaved his way through the crowd which had circled Zoey and the stroller just after she'd been taken off the elevator, near hysteria.

"Please contact Lord Barrett Montgomery, we're in room—"

"Right away, ma'am," the little man said before he scurried off.

Another man, this one larger, with intense, unyielding eyes, used his shoulder to cut a path through the people.

"I'm Hal Lawson," he said as he offered her his big, beefy hand. "Hotel security. Would you please come with me?"

Zoey nodded, tried to smile at the people who had stayed with her in those first few horrifying seconds, then followed Mr. Lawson to an office off the main lobby.

"Have a seat," he said, indicating one of the two chairs opposite a cluttered desk. "Can I get you anything?"

"I asked the other gentleman to contact Lord Montgomery."

The man's expression instantly grew concerned. "You're with the Montgomery party?" he asked.

She nodded. "This is Rachel Montgomery, the earl's daughter. And this is Alex."

"Tell me what happened, Miss...er...?"

"Kincade," she supplied.

"And you are the earl's...?"

Zoey was trying to figure out how to fill in the blank, when Barrett crashed through the door. He looked mussed and out of breath and she wondered if he had run all the way from the suite.

His eyes met hers and he asked, "Are you all right?"

"Fine. Scared."

Barrett's hand fell to her shoulder, offering a reassuring squeeze. "What the bloody hell happened?"

"I saw her," Zoey answered, shivering at the memory. "She's here in the hotel."

Mr. Lawson stepped forward and extended his hand toward Barrett. "How can we be of assistance?" he asked.

"It would seem there is a woman who is quite determined to get her hands on little Alex, here," Barrett said, absently touching the top of the little boy's head. Then, turning his dark eyes on Zoey, he asked, "Was it the same woman you saw before?"

"Yes, but this time I got a better look at her. She's young."

Mr. Lawson insisted that Barrett take a seat as he pulled a form from one of the compartments on a credenza behind his desk. With the shock waning, Zoey became more aware of her surroundings. Mr. Lawson's office was nothing like the rest of the hotel. It looked much like any other office, save for the framed pictures of the security man receiving a hug from Mickey Mouse. The room smelled of stale coffee and drugstore cologne.

"Do you know the lady's name?" he asked Zoey.

"No," she answered. Her strength was fortified when Barrett reached over and covered her hand with his. She drew on his support to keep the sense of utter frustration from consuming her.

"You said she was young?" Lawson asked.

"Early twenties," Zoey supplied. "She had on a hat and big, dark glasses, but her skin was fair. She's definitely tall."

"Are you sure?" Barrett asked.

She met his eyes and said, "Yes. I was standing up this time, so I know for a fact she's a lot taller than I am."

The corners of Barrett's mouth curved down in a definite frown. "That description doesn't fit the woman I saw."

"There can't be two of them," Zoey reasoned. "Alex is only two months old, he can't have that many enemies."

"But his mother must," Barrett countered. "That's the only plausible explanation."

"Now what?" Zoey asked. "We obviously aren't safe here."

"I assure you, Miss Kincade, we can beef up security for the duration of your stay."

"But she's already found us," Zoey argued. "We have to get out of here."

"Mr. Lawson has a point," Barrett said. "Why don't we take up his offer of additional security. It will give us an opportunity to determine the best course of action."

Zoey was still surprised by his position an hour later when they were being escorted back to their suite. On Mr. Lawson's orders, two security guards were positioned outside the only entrances to their rooms. She felt a little better knowing the burly men were there, but still felt strongly that she and Barrett should take the children and leave as soon as possible.

They fed and bathed the babies before putting them on the floor with a selection of soft, cuddly toys. Zoey was back to being afraid of every noise. She jumped when the water pipes sputtered and when the air conditioner cycled on and off.

Barrett came into the living area, carrying two glasses of wine.

"Here, you look like you could use this," he said.

"I can't take this anymore," she said as she allowed her head to fall back against the cushions. "There's no way that woman should have been able to find us, but here she is."

"That does seem an impossible feat," Barrett agreed, taking the seat next to her.

The feel of his large frame beside her was both comforting and tempting. It would be so easy just to lean into him, so easy to ask him to wrap her in the comfort of his arms. But she'd made a stand. There was no way she could back down now.

"Then how did she find us?" Zoey demanded.

"She could have followed us."

"We took a chartered plane. *I* didn't even know what hotel we were going to until we arrived at the front door."

"The point is, she's here," Barrett said in a voice that sounded exasperated. "We have to find some way to safely draw her out."

"What?" Zoey asked, incredulous.

"Listen to me," Barrett said. Placing first his glass, then hers on the coffee table, he took her hands in his. "We won't be comfortable until this woman is caught. She's already taken three chances at Alex."

"Which weren't successful, so he's still in danger."

"We have to use that fact to our advantage," Barrett insisted.

"How?"

"We bring the mountain to Mohammed."

"Come again?"

"We go out, create an opportunity for her to make her move."

"Use Alex as bait? Absolutely not."

"Not bait," Barrett assured her with a sexy half smile that threatened to distract her. "We can arrange for Mr. Lawson's guards to hide the babies while we make a spectacle of ourselves."

"She doesn't want us," Zoey reminded him. "She wants Alex."

"We can fix the stroller to make it look like we've got the babies with us. If we play our cards right, we can flush this woman out."

"Then what?"

"Then we turn her over to the proper authorities and we can get on with our life."

The expression "our life" was probably nothing more than a slip of the tongue. Surely, Barrett couldn't be thinking along those lines.

Zoey was, though. It came to her almost like a flash of divine revelation. Blinking once, she took a long look at him. In spite of the fact that she thought he was a lousy father, she found him a very intriguing man. He seemed like a perfect blend of blatant masculinity tempered by intelligence. What would he be like without that wall? she wondered. She felt certain she knew the answer. No man could kiss her with such exquisite tenderness and not have the capacity for love.

The word reverberated in her brain. Is that what she wanted or expected from him? Zoey swallowed, knowing full well that the answer was yes. She found Barrett so extraordinary, she couldn't imagine wanting another man in her life. He embodied all the qualities she'd ever wanted. He was smart, successful, independent, respectful, funny, and a perfect gentleman. He was also mourning his wife, she reminded herself. If she allowed herself to fall in love with Barrett, she might find herself spending a lifetime alone, or atoning for Alice's sins.

"Well?"

"I'm sorry," Zoey said.

"Are you willing to give it a try?"

"Do you really think the babies will be safe here without us?"

"No."

"Then forget it."

Barrett smiled. "I think the babies will be safe if we plan this carefully."

"Meaning . . . ?"

UNDER AN HOUR LATER, Barrett and Zoey left the suite pushing the stroller. Zoey's heart was pounding in her ears. "Tell me again that this will work."

"We considered everything down to the smallest detail," he reminded her, splaying his hand at the small of her back as he ushered her into the elevator. "Mrs. Cross is well-known to the hotel and certified in every sort of medical emergency. Alex and Rachel will be fine."

"Do you think we left enough bottles and diapers?" Zoey asked. "Maybe we should go and—"

"Hush," he said, placing his finger against her lip.

She tried not to think about the way his finger felt on her mouth. Tried, but didn't succeed, not when her heart had fairly leaped out of her chest in response.

"Those babies are surrounded by more guards than the crown jewels."

"I guess you're right," she said as the elevator doors pushed closed. "It's just that it's the first time I've left them alone."

"You'll get accustomed to it."

"You're awfully cavalier about your daughter's well-being."

He let out an audible sigh. "Are you going to lecture me again?"

"If that's what it will take to get you to change your attitude."

"There's hardly anything wrong with my attitude," he countered.

"You spent more time telling your brother what was happening here than you did consoling your daughter."

Barrett regarded her with something that resembled impatience. "Herbert is capable of carrying on a meaningful conversation. Rachel hasn't a clue what we're up to."

"You could have spent more time with her before we left," Zoey argued. "Was it really necessary to tell Herbert that I had 'gone down in hysterics'?" she asked, quoting that part of his telephone conversation.

"I was only sharing my honest observations," he said dryly.

"Your brother must think I'm some sort of shrinking violet."

"No," Barrett assured her. "He thinks nothing of the sort."

Zoey didn't like the way that sounded. Had Barrett confided something to his brother? Had he even mentioned her before this? It was unrealistic for her to hope that he had told Herbert about her. Barrett had kept his conversation with his brother to such things as estate matters and the occasional mention of Rachel. In fact, now that she thought about it, Barrett had spent several minutes telling Herbert little things about the baby. Apparently, Herbert cared more about the baby than Barrett did, if the litany of answers was any indication. Maybe Barrett would eventually become more like his brother. The thought gave her cause for hope.

"Where are we going?"

"I thought we should go over to Epcot Center. The laser show is later and draws an enormous crowd."

"You really think she'll come after Alex again?"

"If we present her with an opportunity, I believe so."

They took the monorail service to the nearby attraction. An empty car allowed them to lift the dolls in and out of the stroller without anyone getting suspicious.

"Do you think this one barfs?" Zoey teased as she unwrapped her doll for examination.

"Save us, no," Barrett answered.

His features held the eerie yellow glow of the car's interior lighting. Zoey sat back, quietly studying him. Barrett looked so incredibly sexy in his charcoal gray shirt and black slacks. It seemed the perfect combination for their mission. He always seemed to feel comfortable, no matter what the occasion. It was a type of worldliness that Zoey couldn't even begin to fathom. No one in her circle owned his own company or flew to London at the drop of a hat. Hell, none of her friends had more than two bathrooms in their homes. Barrett was so comfortable surrounded by such wealth.

Closing her eyes, she tried to imagine him sitting in her living room. It wasn't possible. This elegant man would probably be horrified to know that her furniture had come from garage sales and secondhand shops. Her clothes were straight off the rack and she didn't have a hairstylist of her own, or any of the other things he took for granted.

"Why the frown?" he asked.

"Just thinking."

"I know this will work," he said as he leaned forward and placed his hand on her knee. The heat from his fingers seared through the thin material of her dress.

"I was actually thinking of something else."

His smile was slow, almost lecherous.

"Not that," she groaned, though that wasn't completely true. She couldn't seem to keep herself from noticing things about him. She was still bowled over by how handsome he was and continually impressed by his commitment to her and Alex, even if she didn't fully understand it. "I was just trying to picture you in my apartment."

"That's a hopeful sign."

"Barrett," she complained. "I meant I was trying to imagine you on my cruddy couch drinking out of a free-with-purchase glass."

His eyebrows drew together above his intense, dark eyes. "Are you calling me a snob?"

"You have to admit, there's quite a difference in our respective socioeconomic pictures."

Nodding, he grinned. "I far prefer mine, don't you?"

"Not all the time."

He seemed startled by her response. "Money doesn't make one happy," he admitted. "But it certainly can make one's life much easier."

"I guess."

"But you're not convinced?"

"Jury's still out," she told him. "I'm really happy with my life. I don't think you can say the same thing."

"Happiness is relative."

"That's what every unhappy person says."

Barrett fell into yet another of his pensive moods. She continued to watch his profile as he stared out the window.

Excitement began to churn in her stomach as soon as they reached the monorail stop adjacent to the park. It was almost dark when they joined a line of patrons moving through the turnstiles.

The air was thick with humidity and Zoey was glad for her loose-fitting dress. Florida in the height of summer was quite oppressive.

If the heat bothered her companion, he showed no sign of it. He walked through the park as if it was the most natural thing in the world for him to do.

Zoey had the stroller, which was in keeping with their plan. It took a great deal of concentration not to look over her shoulder for some sign of the woman.

"Where do we start?" she asked.

"Security said to wait until we get to the countries."

She remembered from the map of the site that the different nations were represented in a circle at the far end of the park. She vowed to come back one day, when she would be able to actually see some of the spectacular displays.

"You're walking too fast," she called.

"Sorry." He slowed until he fell into step beside her.

"Where are the security people?" she asked.

"There's one over there." He gave a slight nod to the left. "And another one behind us."

"I'm getting scared," she admitted. "What if she does something crazy?"

"She's focused on Alex," Barrett reminded her. "She's never threatened anyone on any of her prior attempts to take the baby."

Zoey and Barrett and their twin dolls strolled around the walkway. They made a point of stopping at each sidewalk vendor, intentionally leaving the stroller unattended in hopes of attracting the woman.

"I'm getting tired," she said. "Could we please stop and call the hotel, just to check on the kids?"

"No," he said in that tone that defied challenge.

"You don't have to snap."

Barrett took her elbow and steered her to a vacant bench overlooking the beautiful water and the towering buildings on the opposite side. Two large trees stood guard over the bench, giving the location a certain amount of privacy. He took the stroller and parked it a short distance from the bench, then sat next to her.

"We can rest for a few minutes," he said.

"Good." Zoey slipped her foot out of her sandal and began to massage the sore instep. "This decoy stuff is harder than I thought."

Zoey took her hair and twisted the ends, lifting the hot mass away from her neck. "What are you doing?" she gasped when she felt his lips brush the sensitive skin near the base of her throat.

"I want the woman to think we're distracted." Each word was separated by a feather-light kiss.

"There has to be a better way," she told him.

"I doubt it," he purred.

Zoey's pulse fluttered each and every time his breath spilled over her collarbone.

"We've tried to pretend this isn't happening," he continued, punctuating his remark with a kiss on her ear. "I look at you and I can't think of anything but this."

Barrett pulled her to him, then slid his palms up her arms until he cradled her face in his hands. Using his thumbs, he tilted her head back and hesitated only fractionally before his mouth found hers. Instinctively, Zoey's hands went to his waist. She could feel his muscles stiffen in response to her touch.

The scent of soap and cologne filled her nostrils as the exquisite pressure of his mouth increased. His fingers started to slowly massage their way toward her spine. His fingertips began a slow, sensual counting of each vertebra. Her mind was no longer capable of rational thought. All her attention was homed in on the intense sensations filling her with fierce desire.

With her heart racing in her ears, she allowed herself to revel in the feel of his strong body against hers. As he deepened the kiss into something more demanding, she succumbed to the potent dose of longing.

She began to explore the solid contours of his body beneath his soft cotton shirt. Everywhere she touched, she felt the distinct outline of corded muscle.

When he lifted his head, she had to fight to keep from giving in to her strong urge to pull him back to her. His eyes met and held hers as he quietly looked down, searching her face. His breaths were coming in short, almost raspy gulps and she watched the tiny vein at his temple race in time with her own rapid heartbeat.

"I think I like clandestine activity," he said with a sexy half smile.

"I don't think you *are* thinking," she countered. "This isn't very responsible behavior," she said against the soft fabric covering his broad chest.

"Who says we aren't responsible?" he retorted as his thumb hooked under her chin. "I can't tell you how responsibly I've been taking my cold showers lately."

She tried to ignore the sudden tightness in the pit of her stomach. But she found it harder to ignore the blatant invitation in his inky black eyes.

"I thought we decided not to do this," she reminded him as she scooted away from him.

"That was before you did that thing with your hair," he said in his own defense. "I'm only human."

"You're an animal," she chided, though secretly she was still trying to figure out if his comment about the cold showers was true.

Zoey and Barrett remained seated on the bench, though it wasn't long before a large group gathered around them. Soon, a stunning laser show split the sky. Zoey got so caught up in what was happening that it wasn't until she began to applaud that she realized Barrett still had her hand.

Slowly, she turned her head, fully expecting to see his lopsided grin. Instead, she saw a frown.

"What's wrong?"

"It's apparent that this was a waste of time."

"It was a long shot," she said with a shrug. "Maybe she got scared off back at the hotel."

"Nothing has scared her off before."

"What do you want to do?"

Now she got the lopsided grin.

"Besides that," she said.

Sighing, Barrett got to his feet, pulling her along with him. "There's really nothing left to do but head back."

"I'll get the stroller."

SOMETHING WASN'T RIGHT, he felt it, sensed it. There was no logical explanation for their lack of success. The woman hadn't missed an opportunity before. Then tonight, nothing. It was as if she had somehow learned of their plan. But that wasn't possible. No one knew what they were up to. No one except hotel security.

Zoey was unusually quiet on the ride back. She kept staring out the window, at the blackness. He was beginning to read her body language. She looked so small and frail. Her legs were tucked under her, with only the hint of her bared foot visible.

Maybe she was annoyed that he'd kissed her. That made him frown. He hadn't meant for it to happen. He had fully intended to honor her request, for the time being. However, when she'd raised her arms to adjust her hair, he just couldn't control himself. Closing his eyes, he summoned the memory of how she had looked, seated on that bench, arms raised, breasts pressing against the thin fabric of her dress. Then she'd lifted her hair, filling the night air with her unique scent. Her graceful neck was just too much of a temptation.

"Barrett?"

Shaking free of the memories, he opened his eyes and found her staring at him. "Yes?"

"Are you okay?"

"Yes, why?"

"We walked forever. I was afraid that we might have pushed too much."

"I'm not exactly lame," he said with a small chuckle.

"You are still recovering, though."

"Recovered," he corrected.

"Then why were you sitting there with your eyes closed?"

He saw the concern in her gaze and it touched him. "I was . . . thinking."

"About what?"

"You."

Zoey sat back, putting some distance between them. He wished she wouldn't do that. How could she respond so honestly when he touched her, yet retreat whenever they broached the subject of their mutual physical attraction? Women were too damned complicated.

The lobby was filled with milling tourists, but they were spared the crush of the returning crowd at the elevators. Mr. Lawson took them through the lobby, to the service area.

"Are the babies okay?" Zoey asked.

"I checked not ten minutes ago," he answered. "Everyone was fine."

Barrett watched as Zoey's pretty features relaxed upon hearing the news.

"Take Rachel," she told him when they entered the room where the babies had been hidden away during the pointless outing.

Well, not totally pointless. He'd had an opportunity to share a few minutes alone with Zoey. He had to admit that he'd liked it. What would it be like to have an honest date with the woman? No danger, no fear and no babies.

His daughter whimpered slightly when he lifted her out of the crib. Barrett steeled himself for her cries, but Rachel only wiggled a bit, then buried her little face against his shoulder.

"You're making progress," Zoey whispered.

Mr. Lawson took them up to the suite, using his security pass to open the door. The man flipped a light switch. It took a few seconds for Barrett's brain to register what his eyes were seeing. When it happened, he very nearly dropped the baby.

Chapter Ten

Zoey gasped and felt herself begin to weave as she eyed the near-total devastation. She heard Barrett let out a colorful string of expletives as they stepped over the trash and cushions strewn around the room. The person who had destroyed the room had done it methodically, complete with slashing the pillows and showering everything in a coating of fine down.

"I'll call the police," Lawson said. "Don't touch anything."

Zoey barely heard the man. Her full attention was on a small pile she saw in the far corner. Sidestepping debris, she went over for a closer inspection.

"Oh, my," she cried. "My clothes."

Balancing Alex against her shoulder, she reached out and plucked one of the torn fragments. Everything she had brought to Florida was ripped or cut into small pieces. It chilled her blood to think someone hated her enough to do such a terrible thing.

"Come on," Barrett said gently as he cradled her arm. "Leave it."

"Who would do this?" she asked.

"I don't know."

Barrett, Zoey and the children were given a different room in another part of the hotel. She was beside herself, feeling a strange mixture of fear and intense anger.

"Is there anyone in your life capable of doing this?" Barrett asked when they were alone once again.

"No," she answered as she raked her hand through her hair.

"Think, Zoey. An old boyfriend, anyone?"

"No," she insisted. "I've only had two serious relationships in my life and they both ended amicably."

"Are you sure?"

"Yes," Zoey answered. Falling into a chair, she wrung her hands and nervously tapped her feet while her mind whirled. "What about you?"

Barrett stopped pacing in midstride and stared at her, obviously shocked. "The only person who ever hated me is no longer alive."

The coldness in his voice was echoed in his eyes. "I'm sorry to bring it up," she said, "but you saw our suite. Whoever did that wasn't playing with a full deck. I don't suppose there's any chance that your late wife had a twin?"

"No, thank heavens," he answered. "Alice didn't have any family. I think that was one of the things that attracted her to me."

"What?"

Barrett took a long drink of brandy before he moved to the window. He kept his back to her as he continued, "Alice met my brother, Herbert, when she was traveling in Europe. By the time I was introduced, Alice had adopted my entire family and vice versa. It wasn't until after her death that I realized it wasn't my family she was taken with, it was my family's money. Apparently, greed was a major trigger for her psychosis. And you seem to be forgetting something."

"What?"

"The phone calls started before we met."

"Point," she conceded. "I can't believe I let those calls scare me. Compared to having your entire wardrobe cut to shreds, they were a walk in the park."

"Maybe Lou has had some luck tracking down Alex's father."

LOU TURNER WAS just as frustrated as Zoey when they spoke upon her return one afternoon a few days later. "The Florida police department faxed me a copy of their report this morning. Was it really that bad?"

"And then some," Zoey answered. "I don't know what I'm going to do. I should leave here."

"I hate to say this," Lou said, "but I think you're as safe as you're going to get."

"But what about Barrett and Rachel? I'm so afraid I'm putting them in jeopardy by staying."

"I can put the two of you in a safe house," he said. "But I don't have the manpower Montgomery has at his disposal."

"We're surrounded now," she informed him. "Barrett has someone at every window and door. It's creepy."

"It's smart," Lou countered. "I know this is getting to you, but you're just going to have to hang tough until we get a break."

"My supervisor at Social Services is getting crazy," Zoey told him. "She's making noises about pulling Alex out of my care."

"I know you don't want to hear this, but that isn't such a bad idea."

"Right," she snorted. "He'll be so much safer in an institution with twenty other babies and one residential attendant."

"Is there anything you want me to do?"

"Yes. If Susan has some time . . ."

"I'll give her the new number and tell her to give you a call. Let me know if anything, even something small, happens. Remember, Zoey, no more stunts like that crap you two pulled in Florida."

"Barrett and I have given up playing detective."

She replaced the receiver and went to the refrigerator for a soft drink. Late-August sun poured through the skylights, presenting a serious challenge for the air conditioner. Barrett was locked in his office, doing whatever it was he did when he hid himself away.

Rachel and Alex were sleeping, and thanks to Rosita, the housekeeper, there was nothing much for her to do in the sprawling house. She wandered over to the window and looked longingly at the swimming pool. If things were different, she'd be out there, enjoying the heat of the sun and getting a little exercise, to boot.

No sooner had she come to the window than one of the blasted guards came out of hiding. Startled, she stepped back, but not until she had saluted the emotionless man. As usual, he didn't respond. None of them responded. The security men that worked for Barrett were like little robots. Robots with guns.

"Are you relaxing?"

She shook her head. "I'm losing my mind." Realizing what she'd said, Zoey lifted a hand to her mouth to hide her embarrassment. "I didn't mean—"

"Forget it," he said with a shrug of his broad shoulders.

Barrett was dressed very casually this afternoon. In fact, it was the first time she had ever seen him wearing shorts. His legs were bronzed, masculine and appeared powerful. With his tank top falling off one shoulder and his hair slightly mussed, he could have passed for a regular person, nothing lordly.

When he rummaged in the refrigerator, Zoey was treated to an unobstructed view of his tush. And quite a tush it was, she thought with a wicked little grin. She was still wearing that grin when he turned unexpectedly, catching her in the act.

"Is something wrong, Miss Kincade?" His voice was deep, seductive.

"No." Zoey cringed when she heard the helium-high pitch of her own voice. "Nothing," she added in a more even tone.

"You don't seem yourself," he said as he began walking in her direction.

She took an involuntary step backward. The action didn't go unnoticed, not if his satisfied smirk was any indication, but he didn't slow his pace.

"Barrett," she cautioned as she held up one hand, palm out. "We aren't going to do this."

"I haven't done anything," he purred.

Zoey backed up farther, only to find herself against the cool wall. Barrett kept coming, his intense eyes belying the small smile curving his chiseled mouth.

"Please?"

Without a word, Barrett took the soft-drink can from her hand and deposited it on the nearest table. Then he flattened his palms on the wall on either side of her head.

She could smell his musky cologne and hear his slightly uneven breath. There was a smoldering intensity in his eyes that sent a ripple of desire into the pit of her stomach.

"Please what?"

His warm, mint-scented breath washed over her face. Tilting her head back, she searched his eyes beneath the thick fringe of his eyelashes.

"I've been very, very patient," he said.

Bending at the waist, Barrett leaned forward until his lips barely grazed hers. Wide-eyed, Zoey experienced the first tentative seconds of the kiss through a haze of surprise. The pressure from his mouth increased almost instantly. It was no longer tentative. It was demanding and confident, apparently fueled by the days of accidental touches and meaningful looks that punctuated their tense coexistence.

His hands moved slowly, purposefully to her waist. He slipped his strong fingers beneath the fabric of her top and came to rest just below the swell of her rib cage. Her mouth burned where he incited fires with the expert exploration of his tongue. A sigh inspired by pure animal desire rose in her throat. She was being bombarded with so many sensations at once, each more pleasurable than the last. The callused pad of his thumb brushed the bared flesh at her midriff. His kiss was so thorough, so wonderful that her knees were beginning to tremble.

When he pulled away, Zoey very nearly reached out to keep him close to her. It wasn't necessary; he didn't go far. She listened to the harmony of their labored breathing as he rested his forehead on hers.

"What are we doing?" he said raspily.

"I believe you just kissed me."

"I kissed you. You responded. Why do we fight this, Zoey? Why are we playing this game?"

"It's not a game," she said, feeling sad and lonely all of a sudden. "We both know this isn't such a great idea."

"That," he said as he lifted his head and met her eyes, "is the dumbest thing I've ever heard you say."

Barrett wasn't subtle with his second kiss. There was nothing even remotely sweet about it. This kiss was meant to do one thing, convey desire. Even before he pressed his hardness into her belly, Zoey knew he was aroused as she'd never seen him before. She also knew that she had to keep this from happening, no matter how much she wanted it herself.

"Don't," she said as she placed her hands flat against his chest and gave a little shove. "This is wrong."

"How can you say that?" he countered.

She watched him from behind the safety of her lashes. "I don't do this sort of thing. I don't sleep around for the hell of it."

"Zoey." He said her name on a rush of breath. "I don't want to make love to you for the hell of it."

"Then why?" she asked, truly confused.

He looked at her with eyes so full of tenderness she almost sighed. "I want to make love to you because of you." He brushed his lips across her forehead. "Because of everything you've done for me."

"Gratitude isn't a reason."

"Not gratitude," he insisted as his fingers moved to grip her upper arms. "Because of the things we've shared. The way you've treated both Rachel and me." His lips touched hers. His voice deepened to a husky whisper as he continued, "We've shared more than meals, Zoey. Like it or not, there's more here than just lust. I love the way you fuss over the babies."

He kissed her lightly.

"I love the way you laugh. I love the fire in your eyes when you're angry. I even love the way you've tried to reform me."

"Barrett?" she whispered, feeling her defenses crumble.

"Don't fight me, Zoey, please. I know it will be wonderful between us, and I don't think I can continue as we've been."

"But I need more," she said, still unsure.

He kissed her with equal measures of passion and pleading. "I'll give you everything, Zoey. Trust me."

"You're confusing me," she admitted.

"I'm trying not to," he said quietly. He captured a lock of her hair between his thumb and forefinger. He silently studied the pale strands, his expression dark and intense.

"I don't know what to do, Barrett. I don't want to make a mistake."

"You won't," he promised, his voice low, almost seductive.

The sincerity in his voice worked like a vise on her throat. The lump of emotion threatened to strangle her as the moments of silence dragged on.

"We don't have anything in common," she said finally. "We want different things."

"We've never talked about what we wanted," he countered, his voice rising a notch. "We can do that, Zoey. Later," he said as he scooped her off the floor, cradling her against his hard chest.

Barrett carried her down the hall to his bedroom. As if she were some fragile object, he placed her on the bed, gently arranging her against the pillows.

Zoey remained silent as she watched him shrug out of his shirt before joining her on the bed. Through passion-dilated eyes, she took in the impressive sight of him. Rolling onto his side, Barrett pulled her closer, until she encountered the solid outline of his body. His expression was fixed, his mouth little more than a taut line.

"I'll make it good, Zoey. You'll see," he said as he gently pulled her into the circle of his arms.

It felt so good, so right. She needed this, needed his strength if she was going to make it through this without losing her mind. Closing her eyes, Zoey reminded herself that thanks to Barrett, she and Alex were safe.

She surrendered to the promise she felt in his touch.

Cradling her in one arm, Barrett used his free hand to stroke the hair away from her face. Greedily, she drank in the scent of his cologne as she allowed her fingers to rest against his thigh. His skin was warm, and smooth, a startling contrast to the very defined muscle she could feel beneath her hand. She remained perfectly still, comforted by his scent, his touch and his nearness. Strange that she could only find such solace in his arms. Being in this room with Barrett was enough to erase the fear and uncertainty that had plagued her for weeks. What could be the harm in just a few hours of the pleasure she knew she could find here?

"Zoey?" he asked on a strained breath. He captured her face in his hands, his callused thumbs teased her cheekbones. His brown-black eyes met and held hers, his jaw set, his expression serious. "I don't know if I have the strength to let you get up and walk away from me now. Please tell me this is what you want. Please?"

Using his hands, he tilted her head back. His face was a mere fraction of an inch from hers. She could feel the ragged expulsion of his breath. Instinctively, she flattened her palms against his chest. The thick mat of dark hair served as a cushion for her touch. Still, beneath the softness, she could easily feel the hard outline of muscle.

"I want you so badly," he said in a near whisper.

Her lashes fluttered as his words washed over her upturned face. She needed to hear those words, perhaps even wished for it. Barrett's lips tentatively brushed hers. So feather-light was the kiss that she wasn't even certain it could qualify as one. His movements were careful, measured. His thumbs stroked the hollows of her cheeks.

Zoey banished all thought from her mind. She wanted this, almost desperately. His hands and lips made her feel alive. The ache in her chest was changing, evolving. The fear and confusion were being taken over by new emotions. She became acutely aware of every aspect of him. The pressure of his thigh where it touched hers. The sound of his uneven breathing. The magical sensation of his mouth on hers.

When he lifted his head, Zoey grabbed his broad shoulders. "Don't," she whispered, urging him back to her.

His resistance was both surprising and short-lived. It was almost totally forgotten when he dipped his head. This time, he did more than brush his lips against hers. His hands left her face and wound around her small body. Barrett crushed her against him. Beneath her hands, she could feel the pounding of his heart.

The encounter quickly turned into something intense and consuming. His tongue moistened her slightly parted lips. The kiss became demanding and she was a very willing participant. She managed to work her hands across his chest, until she felt the outline of his erect nipples beneath her palms. He responded by running his hands over her back and nibbling her lower lip. It was a purely erotic action, one that inspired great need and desire in Zoey.

A small moan escaped her lips as she kneaded the muscles of his chest. He tasted vaguely of mint as he continued to work magic with his mouth. Zoey felt the kiss in the pit of her stomach. What had started as a pleasant warmth had grown into full-fledged heat emanating from her very core, fueled by the sensation of his fingers moving along her back, entwining in her hair and guiding her head back at a severe angle. Passion flared as he hungrily devoured first her mouth, then the tender flesh at the base of her throat. His mouth was hot, the stubble on his jaw slightly abrasive. And she felt it all. She was aware of everything—the outline of his body, the almost arrogant expectation in his kiss. Barrett was obviously a skilled and talented lover.

This was a wondrous new place for her, special and beautiful. The controlled urgency of his need was a heady thing. It gave Zoey the sense that she had a primal power over this beautiful man. She found herself a compliant and demanding partner.

Barrett made quick work of her clothes. He kissed, touched and tasted until Zoey cried out for their joining. It was no longer an act, it was a need. She needed Barrett inside her to feel complete.

Poised above her, his forehead glistening with perspiration, Barrett looked down at her with smoldering, heavy eyes. He waited for her to guide him, then filled her with one long, powerful thrust.

The sights and sounds around her became a blur as the knot in her stomach wound tighter with each passing minute, until she felt the spasm of satisfaction begin to rack her body. Barrett groaned against her ear as he joined her in release.

As her heart rate returned to normal, her mind was anything but. She lay there, perfectly still, not sure what to do or say. She'd made love to Barrett with total and complete abandon. The experience was wild, primitive and extremely scary. Her eyelids fluttered as she began to think of the consequences of her rash behavior.

Guilt swept over her like a blanket as she realized the gravity of the situation. Things would never be the same between them.

"Where are you going?" Barrett asked, struggling against her attempt to move out of his arms.

"Back to my room."

"Not bloody likely," he growled as he brushed his lips against her dampened forehead. "Like it or not, Zoey, we're lovers now."

"I'm not sure I like it."

Barrett's sigh was loud and meaningful. "You're having second thoughts, I take it."

Placing her hand beneath her cheek, she nodded against his chest. "Um," she mumbled.

"Why?"

"I'm not good at this sort of thing. I don't make a habit of jumping into the sack with a guy just because—"

"Hush," he interrupted. "I know exactly why we made love."

"You do, huh?" She held her breath.

"It's because of the way we feel about each other."

Was it possible he was feeling the same things she did? Zoey didn't dare hope, not yet. "Desire is a pretty lousy reason for two people to—"

"Not just desire, Zoey," Barrett said with conviction. "It's more than that and I think you feel it, too."

Feel what? That could mean too many things, for her to get her hopes up. "I'm not sure what I feel," she told him honestly.

"We don't have to label it tonight," he assured her. "We have all the time in the world."

To do what? she wondered. "Lou will eventually discover who is behind all this."

"And?"

"Then I go back to my studio apartment in Bethesda and you go back to being an earl."

"Says who?"

Clutching the sheet to her chest, Zoey sat up in order to see his expression. "What are you saying?"

"Simple," he said as his finger came up to trace the contour of her cheek. "I don't want you to go back to your apartment in Bethesda. I want you here with me."

Zoey's heart stopped for a second. "Did I hear you correctly?"

Barrett gave her a small grin. "I thought grand passion was supposed to render one speechless, not deaf."

Slapping his arm playfully, she asked, "Are you telling me that you want to start something here?"

"I believe we've already started," he teased.

"Barrett," she groaned in frustration. "I need to know what you're talking about—specifically."

"Okay. I want you to stay with me."

Zoey was speechless, afraid that if she said something, he might take back his offer.

His chuckle was deep. "Relax."

Zoey blushed furiously. "It won't be easy," she warned.

"Agreed. But things will get better. Especially once you're able to return Alex to Social Services."

Chapter Eleven

"Why did you run out?" Barrett said a few minutes later when he found her in the family room. "And why are you sitting here in the dark?"

"I'm trying to figure out how I could have been so wrong about you," she answered.

"Wrong how?" he asked as he knelt beside her chair.

Grasping the folds of her robe together, Zoey shrugged. "I don't know how you could have been so willing to help Alex, when now you tell me that you can't wait for me to get rid of him."

"You misunderstood my point."

She looked into his eyes, silently hoping that was the case. "What did you mean?"

"I meant it will be easier for us to explore our relationship when we don't have babies coming out of the blasted woodwork."

"That's my job," Zoey countered, feeling the threat of frustrated tears. "I'll always have babies coming out of the woodwork."

Grasping her hands, he held them tightly in his own and quietly searched her eyes. "I understand and support your commitment to little Alex," he began. "Once we get him squared away, we need some time, just the two of us."

"What about Rachel?" she reminded him.

"And her, of course."

"Let me get this straight." Zoey pulled her hands away from him and clasped them tightly in her lap. "I'm supposed to give up my job just so it will be convenient for us to sleep together."

His expression grew dark and dangerous. "You're twisting my words."

"Then, explain them to me."

"We need time together, Zoey." The hardness drained from his expression, replaced by something softer, less threatening. "That can't happen when your time is consumed by other people's children."

"But that's my job, Barrett. It's what I've committed myself to."

"Commitments change," he countered. "Or is it that you've decided you're not interested in pursuing this?"

Blowing an exasperated breath toward her forehead, Zoey said, "I don't even know what *this* is."

He rose abruptly, his fists balled at his sides. "When you figure it out and make your decision, let me know."

"WHAT GIVES?" Susan asked after she had witnessed an hour of Barrett stalking into and out of his office.

"It happened," Zoey admitted.

"It?" Susan parroted. "Capital *I* it?"

Zoey nodded.

"I told you living here wouldn't work. Geez, Zoe, what are you going to do?"

"Make a choice."

Susan's eyes narrowed questioningly. "Choice?"

"Barrett says he wants to explore a relationship."

"Is that what you want?"

Running her fingernail around the rim of her coffee cup, she felt a sigh spill from her tense body. "I think so, but there's a price."

"That's helpful. Just what are you supposed to give up in the name of this glorious exploration?"

"Alex."

"You're joking, right?"

"Well," she amended, "Barrett doesn't think we'll be able to see if things can work between us when I'm preoccupied with other people's children."

"What about his kid? Does he think Rachel will disappear for this process?"

"That's one of the weird things," Zoey said. "He acts like she doesn't exist. I don't know what to do."

"What do you want?"

Meeting her friend's eyes, Zoey thought for a minute, then said, "Him. I want him."

"Enough to give up foster care?"

Lowering her lashes, Zoey shook her head. "I'm not sure. If I did, I could still take care of Rachel."

"But you said you wanted to do this because you wanted to help children in real need."

"Rachel is in need," Zoey assured her. "Barrett still doesn't seem to have any interest in her."

Susan nodded. "Tell me something."

"What?"

"Do you want Barrett, or do you want security?"

"Susan," she cried. "How can you even suggest something like that?"

"Look around. Pretty nice digs."

"He could be poor, for all I care. I don't want his money, I want him."

Susan's smile was slow in coming but when it did, the grin dominated her face. "I think it's finally happened."

Zoey gaped at her friend, uncomprehending.

"You must be in love. That's the only thing I can figure."

"That's crazy."

"I've never seen you agonize about anything like this," Susan argued. "If you didn't love the guy, you would have told him to take a flying leap the minute he so much as suggested you stop fostering."

"I don't know him well enough to be in love," Zoey said stubbornly.

"Bull-tooties," Susan grunted with a dismissive wave of her hand. "I don't like Montgomery all that much. However, if you are in love with the guy, I don't think you should ruin your life by pretending you're not. You could lose him."

"I don't have him." Zoey sighed.

"Right. That's why he looks at you constantly."

"He isn't even speaking to me now."

"He watches when you're not looking. He has all the classic signs."

"The only sign I've seen is an ultimatum," Zoey complained. "You don't ask someone to give up their job if you really love them."

"You do if you're insecure."

A mirthless laugh rumbled in her throat. "Barrett? Insecure?"

Susan shrugged. "His wife did a number on him, Zoey. You're going to have to wade through all that if you really want him."

"This is getting too complicated."

"Not really. Why don't you try a date?"

She met her friend's expectant gaze. "We can't leave the house," she argued. "I don't think—"

"Lou and I can watch the babies for a few hours."

"Excellent idea," Barrett chimed in as he appeared in the kitchen. "Thank you."

Susan's smile was still frosty, but she offered one all the same. "Take her someplace nice, Your Lordship."

"I will."

Susan stood and walked to where Barrett lounged in the doorway. "Don't screw this up," she warned.

HE FELT as nervous as a schoolboy. His fingers seemed unwilling to cooperate so he was making his third attempt at his tie. As if it wasn't difficult enough, he was continually distracted by the sounds coming from the adjoining bedroom. Finally, he slipped his jacket on and checked himself in the dressing-room mirror.

He went to the bar and poured himself a brandy while he waited for her to appear. He tried to busy himself with the day's mail; there was a stack forwarded by his brother, mostly bills associated with the day-to-day running of the family home. The largest bill was for the telephone. There were several calls from an unfamiliar Maryland area code to England. He wondered how long it would take to get those errors corrected.

"I'm ready," Zoey announced.

When he turned, his breath caught in his chest. She looked so different, stunning. The simple black dress hugged her curves and brought about the predictable response in his body.

"You look lovely," he said as he stepped forward.

If the slight tremor in her hand was any indication, Zoey was just as nervous. As she tossed her mane of hair over her shoulder, Barrett was teased by the feminine scent of her perfume. His throat was dry and he knew that was a physical manifestation of his emotional turmoil.

"Shall we?"

They went to one of Washington's finer restaurants, a quaint, dimly lit place with perfect food, prompt service and complete privacy. Zoey was completely charmed by the atmosphere and her host. She was seeing a new side of Barrett, a very irresistible one.

"More wine?"

"No," she said, taking her half-full glass out of his range. "I don't think I can put another thing in my mouth."

"They have a wonderful dessert chef."

"I couldn't really."

"Coffee?"

"Sure," she said with a smile. "You found my weakness."

"One of them," he whispered with a wink.

"Don't make me blush," she pleaded.

Her eyes reflected the flame of the small candle in the center of the table. He watched her as a small army of waiters cleared their table and served coffee in delicately appointed cups.

"This was nice," Zoey said. "Thank you."

"Is that my cue to take you home?"

"No," she answered. "It's really nice to be out in public. I was starting to feel like a prisoner."

"This has been difficult on all of us."

"You, for no reason." She reached across the starched tablecloth and touched the back of his hand. "Thank you."

"I don't want your gratitude, Zoey."

"What do you want?"

Barrett leaned back and stroked his chin. "I want you in my life."

"And Rachel?"

"She's already a part of my life."

"Not your favorite part, though." Knowing the statement was true made her feel sad.

"What do you want from me? I can't help it if I'm not as keen on babies as you are."

"I know that. I don't expect you to be."

"But you do," Barrett countered as he folded his hands on the table in front of him. "You expect me to have the same parental zeal that you possess."

"Zeal?"

He nodded. The action caused a lock of his hair to fall down on his furrowed forehead. "You expect me to react as you do. I can't."

"You could if you tried."

"I don't want to try, Zoey. I want whatever relationship develops between Rachel and myself to evolve from honesty, not because I'm trying to pretend I'm something I'm not."

"Why don't you want to try to be a good father?"

"After all the time we've spent together, do you really think I would allow anyone or anything to harm my daughter?"

"No."

"Do you think I would let her go without anything she needed?"

"No."

"Do you think I would be capable of mistreating her in some way?"

"Of course not."

"Then why do you insist on making me out to be a wretched parent? Why do you insist on making this an issue between us?"

"I want what's best for Rachel."

"Is that it, Zoey? Or am I supposed to become your version of the perfect father?"

"I don't expect you to do anything."

He offered a weak smile. "But you do."

Zoey thought about his comments all the way home. Was she putting up hoops for him to jump through when it came to Rachel? He was getting better with the baby. Barrett could mix formula, change diapers and keep to a schedule. He'd made great strides since that first disastrous day. Now it was more a matter of Rachel avoiding Barrett than the other way around. By the time they reached the darkened house, Zoey had made a decision.

"I think there might be some merit to what you said," she told him as they pulled into the garage.

"Hush," Barrett barked.

"Why? What's wrong?"

"Did you hear that?"

"What?"

"The sound of a car engine being cut?"

"No. Why?"

"Stay here."

"Like hell," she countered, scurrying out of the car right on his heels.

Barrett moved along in the darkness inside the garage. One arm was at his back, holding Zoey safely behind him. When they reached the opening out to the street, Barrett pushed her flat against the wall.

Her eyes were adjusted to the darkness, which helped. Still, she wasn't sure just who or what she was looking for. She did know that the security men were at Lou and Susan's, guarding the babies.

"Should we call the police?" she whispered.

"Wait!"

She stood still while he dropped to his knees, leaned forward and stuck his head outside. A few moments later, he rose, and yanked her back toward the door to the house.

"Call Lou," Barrett said as soon as they were inside.

"What's happening?"

"Just call Lou and then get behind something. Keep your head down until I come back."

"Barrett!" she wailed. "What's going on?"

"We were followed from the restaurant. There's a car parked at the end of the street."

Zoey followed him down the hallway, jogging to keep pace with his long strides. "What are you going to do?" she demanded.

"Just stay put," he called over his shoulder as he went into his office.

Zoey followed him inside and heard the scrape of a drawer being opened, then closed. Then she heard the faint click of metal against metal.

"What are you doing?" she pleaded.

"I'm going to find out what the hell those people want."

"Those people?" she echoed. "You mean there's more than one person and you're going to stage a confrontation?"

"I want this over, Zoey. Don't worry," he said as he brushed a kiss on her forehead. "I'm a perfect shot."

"This isn't the Old West," she argued, frightened by the mere prospect of Barrett running off with a loaded weapon. "That could be two teenagers out there, for all you know."

"I promise not to shoot if they're necking, okay?"

Barrett was moving so fast that it was a struggle to get in front of him. "Please, Barrett. Let's wait for the police."

He grabbed her upper arms and gently placed her off to one side, out of his path. "Call the police like I asked," he said in a deadly calm tone. "I'll be fine."

"Please don't do this," she said again.

Barrett went out though the garage, leaving Zoey alone with her fears. Gathering her wits, she ran back to the kitchen, stumbling once along the way.

Frantic, she grabbed the phone and began pressing buttons. Nothing. Zoey tried again, then began to shake when she realized the phone was dead.

Chapter Twelve

Barrett approached the car by way of the woods lining the secluded street. Luck was with him; the moon dipped behind a cloud just as he neared the vehicle.

Crouched behind a cedar bush, he fingered the gun, checking the position of the safety. He could make out two silhouettes in the car. The driver seemed larger than the passenger.

After taking a deep breath, Barrett sprang forward, allowing his gun to lead the way. He'd taken two steps, when he heard soft footsteps behind him.

In the split second his attention was distracted, the car started. "Stay back!" he yelled to Zoey, then, bracing his legs apart, he took aim and fired once.

Dogs howled and a distant siren screamed in the seconds following the loud blast. The stench of burned rubber mixed with the unmistakable smell of gunpowder.

"Don't shoot!" a woman's voice called out.

Zoey, flashlight in hand, reached his side, panting as she pointed the beam on the now-still vehicle with the shot-out tire. "I called the police. I told then we had the kidnappers."

Slowly, the passenger door opened and two hands popped up. The woman stepped from the car, her eyes squinting against the harsh light. The driver got out next, arms raised high above his head.

A patrol car careened around the corner as lights began flipping on in the scattered homes of his neighbors. Barrett and Zoey stood together no more than ten feet from the couple.

"The phone lines were cut or something," he heard Zoey say.

"How did you get the cops?"

"I used the cell phone in your office."

"Good thinking."

"Who are they?"

"I don't believe it."

"What?"

As Zoey grabbed his sleeve, Barrett watched the patrolman place handcuffs on the two people. Lowering the gun and flipping the safety at the same time, Barrett took Zoey's clammy hand and walked toward the scene.

"I don't believe it," he groaned again.

"What is it?"

Barrett shook his head when he recognized the woman. Lou arrived just as he and Zoey stepped into the strong spotlight of the police vehicle.

The woman scowled at him, while the man appeared shocked and shaken.

"Why the hell did you shoot at me?" he demanded.

"I told you he was unfit," the woman screeched. "I tried to tell all of you."

"What's going on?" Zoey demanded, yanking his sleeve.

"I knew there was something familiar about those eyes. These are the Keatons."

He heard Zoey gasp before she asked, "Rachel's first foster family?"

Lou rolled his eyes and wiped his mouth. "I guess this means we've been chasing our tails all this time, thinking it was about Alex. Great."

"I don't understand," Zoey cried. "Would one of you please explain it to me?"

LOU AND SUSAN ARRIVED early the next morning. Lou looked tired, no doubt due to a very long interrogation of Dave and Patty Keaton.

The four adults, plus Alex and Rachel, gathered in the family room. Barrett seemed more relaxed, as did Lou. Zoey was the only one with lingering questions.

"Did they say anything?" she asked.

Lou nodded. "Plenty. Mrs. Keaton is your caller."

"That little woman?" Zoey asked.

"I never even considered the Keatons." Barrett sighed. "Given what had transpired, I probably should have thought of them straightaway."

"What did transpire?" Susan asked.

"Mr. and Mrs. Keaton came to my room at the hospital shortly after I regained consciousness. They had their attorney draw up papers that would have vacated my parental rights and allowed them to adopt Rachel."

"You're joking?" Zoey breathed in astonishment. "We're not supposed to do that."

Lou took a sip of coffee before he said, "The wife's pretty far-gone. Apparently, she can't have kids and she thought Rachel should be hers."

"It was quite scary," Barrett agreed. "When they came to the hospital, Mrs. Keaton had already begun calling Rachel Amy."

"No wonder you demanded that she be pulled," Zoey said as she took a seat next to him. "I knew there had been a problem with Rachel's first placement, but I had no clue it was that bad."

"I got the impression that Social Services didn't want to make a big deal of it," Barrett said. "The caseworker said it had just been a misunderstanding."

"That's pretty much the tune the Keatons are singing now," Lou told them. "They've copped to the phone calls and the incident at Babies-N-Things, but they swear they had nothing to do with Florida or the grocery store.''

"What happens now?" Zoey asked as she felt Barrett's hand cover hers.

"We shouldn't have too much trouble proving they were in Florida. They'll be arraigned on attempted kidnapping for now. The feds might get involved when we have what we need to tie them to the hotel B and E."

"Thank God." Zoey sighed as she lifted Alex off the floor and kissed his chubby little cheek. "It wasn't you they were after." Zoey smiled, though she would feel better when Lou had completed his investigation and the nasty couple was tried and convicted.

When Susan and Lou left a short while later, the house seemed to take on a completely new aura. She felt happy for the first time in weeks.

"I think I'll take the babies down to the park this afternoon. They've probably forgotten what it feels like to have sunshine on their little faces."

"I've got to run downtown," Barrett told her. His expression was one of mild disappointment. "Do you want to wait until I get back around five?"

"No way," she said with a bright smile. "You go ahead. We'll be fine, right, guys?"

"I don't know," Barrett began with a deep frown. "Are you sure—"

"We're home free, remember?"

"I suppose."

Looking up at him, she studied the concerned lines around his eyes before saying, "They caught the Keatons, Barrett. Now we get to go back to being normal people."

His expression changed immediately. The frown was replaced by a sexy half smile as he took her hands and pulled her to her feet.

He circled her waist with his large hands as his breath washed over her upturned face. "I like the sound of that," he said in a deep, velvety murmur. "What do you say we get a sitter tonight and try again."

"Try what?"

"See if Susan will take the babies overnight."

"Why should I do that?" she answered coyly, feeling a little thrill in the pit of her stomach.

"Trust me," he said as he teased her lower lip with his teeth. "I'll make it worth your while."

Using the cellular phone, Zoey called Susan and made arrangements to leave the children with her again. Susan was all too willing to help out, as she was busily trying to convince Lou that they needed one last child to make their family complete.

Alex and Rachel must have sensed Zoey's good mood, for they were absolutely perfect babies. They slept while she showered and dressed. They ate taking turns and Alex kept his bottle down.

"This will be great," she told them. "I'll get you guys all tuckered out, then ship you off to see Auntie Susan and Uncle Lou."

Zoey stopped and thought about her statement. It was a sobering moment. "I want to be with Barrett tonight," she admitted aloud. "What happened to my commitment to provide constant care?"

Barrett happened. Love happened. There was no denying it now.

After loading the babies into the stroller, she set out for the park a half mile from the house. She passed the spot where the police had outlined Barrett's shell casing with bright orange chalk. She shivered, but refused to allow the Keatons to ruin her first real day of freedom.

"It's hot," she commented as they turned the corner and continued down the slightly uneven sidewalk.

A tan sedan with tinted windows passed as she bent down to straighten Alex's little hat. An odd sensation crept along her spine. Zoey watched the car drive up the street, then make a right turn. She sighed, relieved as she continued to push the heavy stroller.

"I'm paranoid," she told the babies as the sounds of squealing children told her she was nearing her destination.

Milford Park was a beautifully manicured public park at the edge of Barrett's exclusive community. She guessed that a combination of its many attractions as well as its location made Milford a popular place for upwardly mobile mothers and nannies.

Mature trees lined the paved path that meandered along a bubbling creek. It was cool and pleasant and just what Zoey needed after suffering in virtual isolation for so long. The scent of freshly cut grass filled air that was heavy with the sounds of happy children.

"Let's go to the swings," she said after she stopped to read a legend off to the side of the path.

Zoey had gone about ten yards, when she experienced that strange sensation, the one that made the hairs on her neck stand on end.

To salve her frazzled nerves, she stopped and looked around. Several children played in a field, cyclists and skaters whooshed past. Nothing threatening, nothing out of the ordinary.

It's just going to take some time for me to get over this, she thought as she quickened her pace. Arriving at the area specifically designed for infants, Zoey placed each of the babies in a swing and gave a small push.

With Alex and Rachel settled, Zoey took a seat at a nearby picnic table and tilted her face toward the sun. It felt glorious, but she kept her gaze in the direction of the children.

She had been there for about a half hour, when a small boy she placed at around seven came racing up to her. He smelled of sweat and the outdoors as he offered a smile of missing teeth.

"You Kincade?"

"That's me."

"There's a man at the food stand over there." He stopped long enough to point a dirty finger toward a cluster of trees on the opposite side of the park. "He said he was Barrett and for you to come now."

Alarm bells reverberated as she politely thanked the little boy and asked him his name. Jason agreed to wait with her while she called a friend.

"But you gotta hurry," he insisted as she pulled the cellular phone from the diaper bag and called Lou.

He arrived not ten minutes later, driving his unmarked police car along the same path she had used to bring the babies.

"Jason, this is my friend Lou Turner. He's a policeman."

"Neat," Jason replied. "Do you got a gun?"

"Right here," Lou said, patting the holster at the back of his pants.

Jason walked around, his eyes widening when he spotted the weapon. "Neat."

"Jason," Lou began as he knelt in front of the child, "I'm going to make you my special deputy for the day, okay?"

"Do I get a gun?"

"Not your first day on the job."

"When?"

"Soon," Lou fibbed. "But we have to do a little investigating first. Do you know what that means?"

"We find the bad guys?"

Lou nodded. "Right. I need you to take me to where this man is that told you to get Miss Kincade."

Jason lowered his eyes and kicked a pebble near his foot.

"Is there a problem?" Lou asked.

Jason looked up and said, "Do I gotta give the money back if I tell?"

"Nope. It's all yours."

Jason seemed to relax. "I'll show you."

"Wait!" Zoey called. "I'm coming, too."

They set off across the grass field, Zoey pushed the stroller following Lou and the small boy. Jason skipped along, clearly oblivious to Zoey and Lou's shared concerns.

They reached a clearing where a small house served as combination concession stand and covered porch.

"She was right over there," Jason announced.

"She?" Zoey repeated. "I thought you told me a man named Barrett wanted me."

"She told me to say that. She gave me five whole dollars. Am I in trouble?"

"No," Lou said quickly, ruffling the boy's hair.

"Jason Michael Baines!" A shrill voice split the air.

A woman in her early thirties came marching up, looking positively furious.

"Is this your son?" Lou asked as he reached into his pocket to flip out his identification badge.

The woman's anger quickly dissolved into concern and she pulled her son against her. "Is everything all right?"

"Jason was helping me," Lou said, offering the confused child a smile.

"I'm a deputy," he announced proudly.

"Jason, what can you tell me about the lady who gave you the money?"

"She was pretty."

"What about her clothes?"

"They were pretty."

"Jason, help me out here, buddy," Lou begged. "Is there anything you can remember about the lady? What color hair did she have?"

"I don't 'member."

"How about her car? Did she have a car?"

"Uh-huh."

"Good," Lou breathed. "Do you know what kind of car it was?"

"It was big."

"Okay. What about her hands, did she have any rings on?"

"I don't 'member."

"What exactly did she say?"

Jason scratched his head and said, "She told me the lady at the baby swings was named Kincade and that I was 'posed to tell her that Barrett wanted her."

"Anything else?"

"If I did it, I could have the money for my very own."

Zoey shook her head, feeling all the old fears coming back to the surface.

"Thanks, Jason," Lou said. Then he took one of his cards and handed it to the child's mother, telling her to call him if the child remembered anything more.

"Thank you, Jason," Zoey said as the boy started to walk away.

"'Welcome."

"Now what do I do?" Zoey asked as soon as Jason was out of earshot. "Do you think this is related to the Keatons?"

Lou took in a deep breath, shoved his hands into his front pockets and said, "The Keatons have been out on bail since ten this morning."

Chapter Thirteen

"The kid's mother called about fifteen minutes ago," Lou said as soon as they entered his home later that evening.

"Jason remembered something?"

"He said the woman talked funny."

"What's that supposed to mean?" Barrett asked.

Lou shrugged. "I have a feeling Mrs. Keaton probably disguised her voice, like when she used to call you."

"How did they get out?" Zoey asked.

"Their attorney convinced the judge that this was nothing more than a domestic matter."

"That's crazy," Zoey cried. Then, looking at Barrett, she said, "We can't go out. Not now."

"I agree," Barrett said with a nod.

"I think you should go," Lou said.

Zoey turned and gaped at the man. "We can't go running off to dinner with the Keatons roaming free."

"The Keatons didn't return to their house," Lou explained. "If you two are visible, maybe they'll resurface. We'll keep a tail on you. The babies will be safe here with us."

"So, we just wait to see if they turn up?"

The feel of Barrett's hand at the small of her back provided some fortification.

"They are quite clever," he said to Lou. "If they see any sign of the police, I doubt they'll make any sort of move."

Lou fell into a chair and scratched his head.

"I have another suggestion," Barrett said.

Zoey braced herself, sure she wouldn't like what was about to come out of his mouth.

"What if we play it totally low-key? No police until after we've flushed them out."

"Too dangerous." Lou dismissed the suggestion with a shake of his head.

She watched as Barrett's expression hardened to match the resolve in his voice. "We're talking about my child's well-being."

"And yours and Zoey's," Susan countered.

"I can assure you, I am fully capable of seeing that everyone comes through this safely."

Zoey reached out and took his hand. She remembered vividly how easily Barrett had handled their last confrontation with the Keatons. But it was something entirely different that caused her to offer the man her show of support. His concern, no, the fierceness with which he was willing to protect Rachel, was what had sent her over the edge. She knew then that she loved him. She also knew that if they were ever going to make anything of their relationship, they would have to get out from under the threat the Keatons posed.

"This can work, Lou," she said with conviction. "If the Keatons think we've been lulled into a false sense of security, they'll definitely make a move."

"For the babies," Susan observed.

"Then we can do what we did in Florida," Zoey said excitedly. "Barrett and I can make it look like we've got them with us."

"I thought that didn't work in Florida," Lou reminded her.

It was apparent by her friends' expressions that Lou and Susan didn't share her enthusiasm for the idea. Chancing a look at Barrett, Zoey felt bolstered by his reassuring smile.

"This will be easy," Zoey insisted. "Instead of going to dinner, we'll pretend to take the babies back to the house. All we have to do is sit and wait for the Keatons to show themselves."

"And what will you do when and if they show?" Lou asked.

Barrett answered. "Call and make arrangements for your men to get into position ahead of us. They can hide in the woods."

"This could work," Lou acknowledged grudgingly.

"You're putting Zoey in danger," Susan argued.

"Not really," she insisted. "Barrett can handle a gun and I'm pretty good with a knife." Zoey and Barrett shared a private smile.

"This isn't a joke," Susan wailed.

"I know that. I just don't see any other way."

Susan placed her hands on her hips. "You get the security guys back. You stay in the house and you let the department find the Keatons."

"I don't want to go back to that," Zoey explained. "I don't want to spend weeks and weeks living in fear like some sort of prisoner."

"I think you're all nuts," Susan announced, tossing her hands in the air in a gesture of frustration. Then, leveling her gaze on her husband, she added, "And you'd better think of something else before these two go off and get themselves hurt."

Lou sighed. "I'm not thrilled with the idea, but I don't see how it's all that different from me telling them to go home and I'll post a guard. The only difference is that the babies will be here, where those loony folks can't get to them."

"You have all lost your minds," Susan grumbled.

"Maybe we have," Barrett said a little while later when they were seated in his car, heading to his home with two stuffed animals occupying the car seats. "I should have insisted that you stay behind with the Turners."

"It wouldn't have worked," Zoey told him. "The Keatons know that the babies are usually with me. If we were to split up, there's no telling which one of us they would follow."

"As soon as we get to the house, I want you to get into the cellar and stay put."

"And what will you be doing?"

"Watching."

Zoey placed her hand on his wrist. "Lou was really specific. Any sign of trouble and we're supposed to call for help."

"We'll see," Barrett replied.

"You were right," she said after a brief pause.

"About what?"

"About me trying to mold you into my version of a perfect father. I know now that you love Rachel. It isn't my place to tell you how to express that love."

"I didn't want Rachel," he said in a quiet voice. "I didn't want children."

"Why?"

"I'm just not comfortable with children. They can be quite frightening, you know."

"And wonderful," Zoey reminded him. "How do you feel now?"

"I've warmed to the notion of being a father," he answered. "I'll probably never live up to your expectations, but I think I can do a competent job."

"You just need to lighten up," she said. "Once she starts to talk and respond more, I think she'll have you eating out of the palm of her hand."

"Probably," he admitted. "It was like that with Jenny."

"Your sister?"

"Half sister, actually. My father's child with his second wife. I was twelve when she was born. We all spoiled her terribly, I'm afraid. I often wonder if that might not be the reason why she has so many difficulties now."

"I'm sure she'll be fine," Zoey offered. "A lot of people who are showered with attention as children have a tough time when they go out into the real world. If you're used to being the center of the universe, it's pretty hard to accept the fact that you're really no different than the next guy."

"That's what Herbert keeps telling me."

"Are they close?" Zoey asked.

"Very. Herbert and Jenny share a passion for the estate, the family history, and all things associated."

"And you don't?"

She watched him shrug. "I respect my family's history but I prefer making my own way."

Barrett pulled the car into the garage and cut the engine. "Remember what I said," he cautioned. "I want you to hide yourself away the minute we get inside."

"We'll see," she hedged as she opened her door.

Zoey stepped out of the car and felt something hard stab painfully into her ribs. She opened her mouth to scream, when a hand clamped across her face.

She tasted leather and her own fear as she watched in horror as Barrett and a man in dark clothing struggled. Zoey's first thought was to go to his aid. She jerked her body, but went still when the voice at her ear said, "Don't move or I'll have to kill you."

Zoey winced when she saw the man fighting with Barrett raise a hand with a gun in it and smash Barrett squarely in the temple. He folded like an accordion, slumping between the car and the garage wall.

"Get her to turn off the alarm while I drag him in."

The accent was familiar, as were the man's eyes. Shocked, scared and very confused, Zoey did exactly as instructed by the tall, red-haired woman.

"What do you want?" she asked after she'd been pushed into a chair and Barrett had been dragged to a place by her feet.

Ignoring her question, the man kept his gun pointed on Zoey while he spoke to the woman. "Get the kid out of the car and head for the airport."

Nodding, the woman disappeared into the garage.

The man was only a foot or so away and Zoey silently watched him, trying to memorize every detail.

Barrett groaned and began to rise. The man came over and delivered another blow to his temple. Zoey made a small, frightened noise, and tears came to her eyes when she saw blood spilling from a crease at Barrett's forehead.

"You're gong to kill him," she shouted as she moved to help him.

"Back off!" the man cautioned, waving the gun at her.

"He's hurt."

He came over and grabbed her arm, his fingers painfully digging into her flesh. "Shut up and stay put," he commanded before roughly tossing her back into the chair.

"She isn't bloody there," the woman announced as she stormed back into the room.

Both intruders turned angry dark eyes on Zoey. The woman spoke first. "What have you done with Rachel?"

"I don't believe this," the man shouted.

Zoey jumped as he began to pace, the gun flailing about in his grip. She flinched when he moved toward her, his expression wild and threatening.

"Where is she?"

"I . . . don't know what you're talking about."

She cried out when the back of the man's hand stung her cheek with enough force to nearly knock her from the chair.

"Don't play with me, Zoey."

His eyes flashed and his smirk deepened when she reacted to the use of her name. "Yes, I know all about you, so tell me where the blasted kid is."

As she hesitated, the man slowly moved the gun until it was pointed directly at Barrett's head.

"I'll tell you," Zoey cried. "Don't hurt him."

"I knew this was a bad idea," the woman cut in angrily. "Now we'll have to deal with her, as well."

"Shut up, Jenny."

"Jenny?" Zoey repeated in astonishment. Then everything seemed to click into place. It explained why the man and the woman seemed so familiar. "You're Barrett's sister," she said to the woman.

"Thanks a bloody lot," she snapped at the man.

He glared at Zoey as his mouth pulled into a tight, angry line. "It doesn't matter," he insisted. "You won't say anything, will you, Zoey?"

"No...no."

"Good." He turned to Jenny and said, "Hold your gun on Rhett. Miss Kincade and I shall have a little discussion about what she's done with the baby."

Yanked to her feet, Zoey almost fell as he dragged her across Barrett's still form. The hard edge of the countertop bit into her back as he loomed above her.

"Here's what we're going to do."

Zoey swallowed and nodded. "Anything. Just don't hurt Barrett."

His smile was a cruel, mocking gesture that made her shiver.

"Jenny will stay here with him while you take me to where you've hidden Rachel."

Think! her brain screamed. There has to be a way out of this.

"I'll take you to the baby, Herbert," she said as she rose slowly. Hopefully, she could think of a way to alert the police. Something that would cause them to follow her.

His smile was purely evil. "Very good, Zoey. Rhett said you were bright." He used the gun to direct her toward the door. Glancing once at Barrett's still-unconscious form, Zoey quickened her pace.

"Wait!" Herbert barked.

With Jenny guarding her, Herbert went over to Barrett and pulled off his jacket. Shedding his own,

Herbert put on Barrett's jacket and mussed his reddish hair. "Just in case someone is watching," he said to Zoey.

Herbert wasn't quite as large as Barrett, but there was enough similarity that Zoey knew he could fool anyone watching from a distance.

They moved into the garage, where Herbert retrieved the keys that had apparently fallen from Barrett's hand in their struggle. "You drive," he instructed.

Zoey slipped behind the wheel and started the engine with Herbert and his gun as passengers.

"Wait," he said as she began to ease the car down the driveway. Using the gun, Herbert flipped the switch for the headlights. Then, taking the barrel and slowly dragging it along her arm to her shoulder and finally, to her cheek, he said, "I'm sure that was just an oversight on your part."

"It was," she lied.

"No more accidents."

"What about Barrett?" she asked.

His grin was slow, purposeful. "If we're not back in an hour, dear Jenny will shoot him."

Chapter Fourteen

"What are you looking at?" Herbert growled.

"Nothing," Zoey insisted.

Herbert turned in the seat and checked out the back window of the car. "You'd better not try anything creative, Zoey."

"I'm not," she managed to get out over the lump of fear in her throat. "I don't understand why you're doing this."

Herbert chuckled. "The usual reasons."

"Money?"

"And power."

Zoey purposefully made a wrong turn and silently prayed that Herbert wasn't familiar with the area. "Why do you want Rachel?"

"She's Barrett's heir. That was Alice's idea."

"Barrett said his wife was the one who had wanted the baby."

Herbert made a derisive snorting sound. "Alice didn't want a baby. Rachel was her insurance policy for when Barrett was eliminated."

Zoey made another wrong turn. "I don't understand."

"Alice was supposed to kill Barrett and make it look like an accident."

"What does that have to do with you?"

"I introduced Alice to my dear brother. I knew her mental history and I knew from the time that I...spent...with Alice that she would do anything for money. Without Rhett, I inherit."

Zoey swallowed as the meaning of his words began to sink in. "You must really hate him."

"Not quite. I just have no intention of sitting back while he sells off my heritage."

"What?"

"He's completely seduced by America. It's only a matter of time before he decides that the Montgomery estate is no longer worth his time. He can sell off the lands and leave Jenny and me in the lurch."

"He wouldn't do that," she said, hoping she might be able to appeal to whatever reason he might have left. "Barrett is very proud of your family."

"I *am* the family," Herbert thundered. "Yet I'm denied the title because of an arbitrary matter of birth order. I was the one who stood by Father's side. I have always handled things while Barrett turned his back to pursue his own interests."

"Can't Barrett resign or something?"

"I want the title in my own right."

Zoey drove farther into the hilly terrain. Her spirits fell when she acknowledged that she wasn't being followed. The police couldn't help her, or Barrett, or Rachel.

"You're running low on time, Miss Kincade."

"Let me keep Rachel," Zoey pleaded. "I'll raise her and she'll never have to know about—"

"No loose ends this time," Herbert yelled. "Rachel has to disappear if people are to believe Barrett's tragic suicide."

"What about me?" Zoey asked. "Are you going to kill me, too?"

"I'm afraid that is unavoidable," he said. "I'll have to tell the authorities that my dear brother, distraught and unbalanced, killed his lady friend and then turned the gun on himself. I'll take Rachel back to England and deal with her there."

"Then why should I take you to Rachel if you're going to kill me, regardless?"

"Because I'll find her eventually and when I do, I'll be forced to kill whomever she's with. Your call, Miss Kincade. If I had to guess, I'd wager you left the baby with your friend Susan. The one Barrett isn't fond of. Am I correct?"

Chewing her bottom lip, Zoey was quickly realizing that she was no match for this man. She had to warn Lou and Susan, and she couldn't do that if she was dead. Think!

But she couldn't put Susan and her family in danger. Zoey considered slamming on the brakes or driving them off the road. That might deter Herbert, but she still had Jenny to think about.

Barrett. Her heart ached when she thought of how he had looked, lying there motionless on the floor.

"I believe," Herbert said as he leaned across the console and spoke into her ear, "you're being uncooperative, Zoey. If Jenny doesn't hear from me in the next twenty minutes, dear Rhett is dead."

The plan that materialized wasn't great, but it was the only thing she could think to do. Now, she only had to hope that it worked. If not, the consequences could be disastrous. She would wait until Herbert was almost to the door, then she'd lie on the horn and begin screaming. Lou, she felt certain, was more than capable of protecting his family.

Slowing the car as she turned down Susan's street, Zoey fought against the rush of adrenaline pumping through her system. She needed to remain calm. Her timing and her reflexes were critical if her plan was to work.

Cutting the engine, she turned to her captor and said, "Rachel is inside there."

"Let's go."

"You have the gun," she argued. "Susan won't give you any trouble."

"And I wouldn't dream of leaving you behind."

"I won't run," she promised. "You can take the keys."

He snorted and poked her with the gun. "Seven minutes, Miss Kincade. Seven minutes and Rhett dies."

"Susan will know something's wrong," she told him. "She'll take one look at me and—"

"I don't have time for this," Herbert snarled. "Get moving."

Zoey's heart and mind raced as she walked slowly toward Susan's door with Herbert at her side and his gun in her back. There had to be something she could do to thwart him.

"Press the doorbell," Herbert growled against her ear. "And remember, I won't hesitate to shoot you."

"Susan isn't stupid," she whispered. "She'll wonder what I'm doing with you."

"You'll simply tell her that I'm Barrett's brother, over from England, and I just couldn't wait to see my niece."

"You don't have to do this," Zoey pleaded one last time.

Her hand was shaking so violently that she had trouble with the bell. Her plan hadn't fully evolved, when Susan opened the door wearing a bright smile.

Zoey widened her eyes, trying to communicate fear, danger and the rest of the emotions bottled inside her tense body.

"Hi, Zoey. Come on in."

Zoey made a face at her friend, but Susan didn't pick up on it. She simply stepped back from the open door and ushered them in with her hand.

"Freeze!" Lou shouted at the same instant Zoey felt Susan reach out and pull her to the floor. Bullets ricocheted above her head, and she clamped her hands over her ears. Something heavy fell on her, forcing the breath from her body.

A second later, it was quiet and the weight was removed. Zoey was still, trying to get both her brain and her body to function normally.

"Zoey?" Her name was an urgent whisper.

Rolling onto her side, she looked up into Barrett's worried eyes. "You're okay?" She blinked. Then, looking around, she said, "Is everyone okay?"

He nodded as he lifted her into his arms. Beside them, Lou helped Susan off the floor.

"What happened?"

Barrett smiled down at her. "The cops were suspicious when they saw the car leave."

Glancing at the gash on his forehead, she asked, "Jenny?"

"We'll talk about it later," he said as he brushed some stray strands of hair from her tearstained cheeks. "I'm so glad you're all right. I can't tell you how frantic I've been just sitting here waiting."

"You were waiting for me?"

"Always," he said just before his mouth claimed hers.

"IT'S OFFICIAL," she said, rallying against the threat of tears. "I have to surrender Alex immediately."

"You knew this was part of it when you started," Barrett said in an attempt to comfort her. "I'm sure he'll be fine."

Zoey sucked in a breath and leaned into him, burying her face against his chest. "They won't even tell me her name."

"She's a friend of Alex's mother," Barrett reminded her. "Alex knows her."

"They're suspending my license, too."

"I'm sorry." He patted her back.

"It's probably for the best," she said. "I hate the thought of giving Alex back. I know it's the right thing to do but it really hurts."

"We'll all miss him," Barrett soothed. "He's a great kid."

"Why did I ever think I could do this?" Zoey asked as she placed the last of Alex's belongings into a bag.

Barrett had taken the babies out to the car. At least he would be with her when she delivered Alex to Social Services. Her heart was heavy as she lifted the last of his little T-shirts and brought it to her nose. She breathed deeply, drinking in the baby scent that would be her last reminder of little Alex Spears. It was amazing that she had gotten so attached to the child in six short weeks. The thought that she would never see him again caused tears to well in her eyes.

She stopped short when she rounded the corner to the kitchen. Barrett, his dark eyes watery, was hugging the little boy.

He looked up, meeting her eyes. "I'm glad they're suspending your license," he said with a tremor in his voice. "I don't think I have the strength to do this more than once."

"Me, neither," she agreed as she moved to stroke the soft brown fuzz covering Alex's head. "We'll never know what color his hair is, or how tall he gets, or if he's happy." The tears fell in earnest now. The three of them stood together for the final time.

The mood was somber as they headed toward the state agency. Barrett remained with her as she carried Alex to the appointed office and delivered him to the waiting caseworker. As soon as Alex had been taken from her arms, Barrett handed Rachel to Zoey and the three of them embraced when Alex was spirited from the room.

"You okay?" Barrett asked in a voice choked with emotion.

"Not really," she admitted as they walked toward his car. "I've known this day was coming for two weeks and I never dreamed it would be this painful."

Barrett helped her put Rachel into her car seat, then held the door until she tucked her skirt against her leg. He got in beside her, but didn't immediately start the engine. "I owe Alex a great debt."

"He was a special little boy," Zoey agreed.

"I'm beginning to know how the Keatons must have felt when I insisted that Rachel be taken away from them."

"You did the right thing," Zoey assured him. "Mrs. Keaton needs help."

"Lou said there were hundreds of pictures of Rachel in the cabin where they found them."

Zoey placed her hand on his leg and met his gaze. "Don't worry, Barrett. She's safe now."

Barrett glanced over his shoulder at the sleeping baby. Zoey saw the flash of genuine emotion in his eyes and could almost read his pain.

"I can't believe how close I came to losing both of you," he said.

"But you didn't," she reminded him. "We're both safe and sound."

"And very special to me," he said in a soft, barely audible voice. "I didn't realize just how special until I came to with Jenny's gun in my face."

"Don't."

He shook his head and wrapped his fists around the steering wheel. "I've lost my father and my brother. Jenny will probably spend the rest of her life in jail. You and Rachel are my life, Zoey. Thanks for not giving up on me."

"Thanks for suggesting I give up foster care."

He winced and said, "I have no right to ask that of you. But—" he turned and met her eyes "—I don't know if I can do this again. There has to be something we can do to help these kids without going through this torture."

"I'd like that," Zoey said.

"We'll work on it," he agreed before he started the car.

Zoey was still feeling melancholy later that night. She chased a bit of chicken around on her plate. Barrett did the same, making a polite show of eating the meal she'd prepared. Rachel was in the family room, happily rocking in the new baby swing they had purchased that afternoon as a distraction.

Zoey was distracted in another way, as well. She and Barrett had lived platonically since the death of his brother and the arrest of his sister. Now that Barrett seemed to have placed a new importance on family, she couldn't help wondering if she was included in his future. He hadn't tried to touch her in a couple of weeks, nor did his kisses hold the same passion. She didn't know if it was the trying circumstances of their ordeal or simply the fact that he no longer wanted her.

"I think Rachel needs to be changed," Barrett said without meeting her eyes.

"Do you want me to do it?" she asked.

"Please."

Zoey lifted Rachel out of her swing and carried her into the nursery. She experienced a pang of sadness when she entered the room. She missed Alex.

With one hand on the squirming baby, she reached into the lower compartment of the changing table. Her hand encountered something out of place.

Feeling the squared edges, Zoey grasped the object in her hand and pulled it out for a look. "What is this?"

She tried not to get overly excited at the sight of the small box covered with elegant wrapping paper and tied with a small gold ribbon. After re-dressing Rachel, she carried the unopened present to where Barrett was waiting at the table, wearing a very expectant look.

"Know anything about this?" she asked, waving the box.

"I might have an idea or two."

Zoey handed Rachel to Barrett and hesitated, fully expecting the child to scream. Rachel surprised them both by settling happily into her father's arms.

"Are you going to open it?" Barrett urged. His wide grin was infectious.

"Don't you want me to try and guess what's inside?"

"I want you to open the bloody thing," he said. "Rachel does, too."

"Is this from you, or from Rachel?"

"It was a team effort, of sorts."

Zoey leaned against the edge of the table just a few inches from Barrett. Slipping a fingernail inside the fold of wrapping paper, she began to slowly break the seal of the tape.

"Good heavens, woman," Barrett scoffed as he took the box from her and ripped the paper in one easy motion. "Here."

Accepting the small blue velvet box, Zoey warned herself not to expect too much. So what if it appeared to be a jeweler's box. It could be a pin. It could be earrings.

It could have been, but it wasn't. "Oh, Barrett!"

"She likes it," he said to the baby. "I knew we had great taste."

She touched the tip of her finger to the top of the huge diamond ring. It wasn't fancy or gaudy. It was elegant and classy, just like Barrett.

"This is where you make yourself scarce," he said to his daughter before he took her over to the swing, gently placed her in it and gave a gentle push.

"Now," he said as he placed his hands on Zoey's shoulders.

For several long, silent seconds, he simply looked deeply into her eyes. The look was so tender it made her heart skip.

Barrett took the box from Zoey and pulled the ring free of its packaging. Taking her hand, he lifted her finger and began sliding the ring into place. "I love you."

She pressed a kiss into his chest, then tilted her face upward. "I love you."

"Then, for the sake of our daughter, I think we should get married."

"Our daughter?" she repeated.

Barrett nodded and sighed. "You're right. I stand corrected."

Zoey held her breath when she saw the seriousness in his expression. A second later, a grin curved his chiseled mouth. "I meant to say, our *oldest* daughter."

"What are you saying, Barrett?"

"You aren't usually this dense," he teased as his hands moved behind her back. He locked his fingers behind her and pulled her fully against him. "I'm asking you to marry us."

"Us?"

"I checked with Rachel, and she's quite high on the notion."

"But what about—"

Barrett silenced her with one look. "I want to marry you and have children with you. I want us to grow old together and have grandchildren. So," he breathed, "what do you say?"

Smiling up at him, she tilted her head to the side and asked, "If I marry you, am I in line for the British throne?"

Barrett shook his head before claiming her mouth.

BRIDE'S BAY RESORT

UNLOCK THE DOOR TO GREAT ROMANCE AT BRIDE'S BAY RESORT

Join Harlequin's new across-the-lines series, set in an exclusive hotel on an island off the coast of South Carolina.

Seven of your favorite authors will bring you exciting stories about fascinating heroes and heroines discovering love at Bride's Bay Resort.

Look for these fabulous stories coming to a store near you beginning in January 1996.

Harlequin American Romance #613 in January
Matchmaking Baby by Cathy Gillen Thacker

Harlequin Presents #1794 in February
Indiscretions by Robyn Donald

Harlequin Intrigue #362 in March
Love and Lies by Dawn Stewardson

Harlequin Romance #3404 in April
Make Believe Engagement by Day Leclaire

Harlequin Temptation #588 in May
Stranger in the Night by Roseanne Williams

Harlequin Superromance #695 in June
Married to a Stranger by Connie Bennett

Harlequin Historicals #324 in July
Dulcie's Gift by Ruth Langan

Visit Bride's Bay Resort each month wherever Harlequin books are sold.

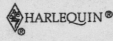

HARLEQUIN®

BBAYG

Bestselling authors

ELAINE COFFMAN RUTH LANGAN

and

MARY MCBRIDE

Together in one fabulous collection!

OUTLAW Brides

Available in June wherever Harlequin
books are sold.

HARLEQUIN ®

OUTB